UNDAUNTED

OPERATION MARRAKESH
BOOK 6

BLAZE WARD

ALSO BY BLAZE WARD

The Science Officer Series

Start with: The Science Officer

The Jessica Keller Chronicles

Start with: Auberon

CS-405 (Command Centurion Kosnett, part of Jessica)

Start with: Queen Anne's Revenge

First Centurion Kosnett (sequel to Jessica)

Start with: Encounter at Vilahana

Additional Alexandria Station Stories

Alexandria Station Collection

Handsome Rob (Alexandria Station Universe)

Start with: Can't Shoot Straight Gang

======================

Corsac Fox

Start with: Flight of the Corsac Fox

Operation Marrakesh

Start with: Trial by Leviathan

Captain Daring

Start with: Revoked

The Hunter Bureau

Start with: Mirrors

Fairchild

Start with: Fairchild

Last Stand

Start with: Lost Dreams

The Lazarus Alliance

Start with: Escape

Shadow of the Dominion

Start with: Longshot Hypothesis

Star Dragon

Start with: Birth of the Star Dragon

Kincaide's War

Start with: The Eden Package

Star Tribes

Start with: Winterstar

ACTION-ADVENTURE

Pacific Force

Start with: Pacific Force

The Red Branch

Start with: Night Strike

Swordmistress Zhen

Start with: Traveler From The West

FANTASTICAL

The Gunderson Case Files, Volume 1

Augustus Derlyth, Occult Detective

Start with: Ill Tidings

PRELUDE

Log: Directorate Cruiser, Tactical Transport Marrakesh (CTT)
Station: Horwin
Attached Special Mission Modules
A) Courier
B) Monitor: Escort
Mission: Diplomatic Transport
Project: W84-CK6F43V73
Security Clearance: 4+

1

—————

Captain Padraig Boru was a little apprehensive to be suddenly summoned to the *A'Zedi* Intelligence Services main Bureau.

No warning. Alone.

A note hand-delivered at the deck airlock for his hands only, necessitating waking him up to receive it, then to have just enough time to shower, shave, and accompany the woman to a nearby shuttle that probably set a new record for fines accumulated in a controlled flight zone, save that Padraig knew they would all vanish.

Chance had been awake and minding the store. Her look as he left had covered everything she would be doing to get the ship ready to travel, because she had been doing this with him long enough to understand what such a summons implied.

The waiting room had not changed. Even with two hours yet until sunrise, there were a handful of older men and women on the other side of the counter, civilian dress to remind you that they didn't care what your military rank was because you couldn't give them orders.

Padraig had just barely had time to sit and take two breaths when the door behind them opened and the Permanent First Secretary, Madam Mariami Gelashvili, appeared.

"Captain, thank you for being so prompt," she announced to the empty space. "Come."

He was up on her first syllable and in motion. Normally, the woman was charm and sophistication itself, but he could see stress in her eyes, even from here.

They got back to her office and she threw herself into her seat.

Padraig flinched when he recognized the other woman seated on this side of the desk.

"Close the door and sit," Gelashvili ordered.

Padraig did, wondering what had happened that he had one of the Directors of the *Sovereign Collective Directorate of A'Zedi* **itself** seated close enough that he could hear her breathing.

Thalia Amano. He only knew her face because he was in *Intelligence* these days, however unofficially, and she was one of a dozen or so power players at the very top.

The VERY top.

"Reports suggest *Marrakesh* could put to sea quickly, Captain?" Gelashvili asked.

"Time to load a pod, normally measured in hours if we do it slowly and carefully," he replied. "Food, fuel, and supplies can be loaded simultaneously. Or we could launch as soon as I hit the deck and handle all that somewhere else, ma'am."

They'd just come off a simple cargo run to the rimward border. Hauling things on a ship that was at least somewhat armed in areas where trouble occasionally happened, but nothing had bothered them this time.

Not every mission was life and death, even in the middle of the larger war.

"I will need a permanent replacement Gunner," he appended after a moment.

"I'm sorry Squire Misra didn't work out," the Secretary offered. "On paper, a perfect fit, but as you noted, a bit too aggressive for your needs. Assuming the meaning of the term *murderhobo* translates."

Padraig grimaced, but nodded.

"Aggressive can be good," he temporized. "She was simply unprepared for the number of times and ways we had to act subtly and outside of all normal military regulations. On a Line Command ship with a strict disciplinarian in command, I believe she would thrive. Ambiguity was her nemesis here."

"And Intelligence work is frequently the height of ambiguity," Gelashvili agreed. "I have someone who was not necessarily considered a good fit at the time, but who brings a raft of secondary skills and expertise that I believe will be useful for your coming mission."

Then she pointedly turned to Director Amano. Padraig did the same.

Gelashvili was tall and somewhat pale compared to the rich, dark browns common in *A'Zedi*. She looked more like someone from the *United Technocracy of Wronlori*, which he presumed had been a useful thing when she'd been younger, because the woman was a spy.

The Director, however, had skin somewhere between umber and ochre. Not as red as walnut, but not as gray as mahogany. A light bronze, if he could parse that difference.

Deeply brown eyes. Black hair that looked natural, in spite him guessing her age around forty-five.

Intelligent face, but he wouldn't call it friendly by any stretch.

"I have been *read in* on your history and operations,

Captain," she began in the kind of quiet voice that sucked you in to stillness to listen.

A natural orator, which made sense as a Director of the *Directorate* itself.

And she used the technical phrase *read in*, which was from intelligence operations and meant that someone had been given specific access to previously compartmentalized information that even the Directors didn't usually need to know.

Padraig nodded and waited as she watched him.

"This mission will be rated at least a Four on the Security Clearance chart," she continued, again pausing to watch him nod once.

The mission last year to rescue the Intelligence Patrol Cruiser *Northwind* from behind enemy lines had been the first time he'd ever encountered a Five in his entire career. Four was only slightly less frightening.

Especially considering the company.

Padraig stayed calm.

"The Supreme Autocrat of *Traisa* has been in secret contact with the *Directorate*," Amano continued. "He wishes to retire and go into permanent exile. The *Directorate* is willing to assist him in this task."

Padraig managed to keep his jaw from falling open. Barely.

In the current War of the Fourth Alliance, it was *A'Zedi* and the *Holy Imperium of Copez* against *Wronlori*, with the *Enlightened Tyranny of Traisa of Traisa* generally neutral, though they had previously allied with either side in previous incarnations of a war that had been running hot or cold for over a century at this point.

And he wasn't aware that Supreme Autocrats *could* retire. All of them that Padraig was aware of had died in office, with most of them being helped along at the end by their replacements.

Unwillingly.

"And my mission, Director?" he asked her directly.

At the end of the day, he was just the guy taking orders from people like these two women.

"*Marrakesh* has experience as a diplomatic transport, Captain," Amano replied, harking back to the mission to Monsach.

And Governor Jamy Hesell, who had sent Padraig a birthday card. Along with suggestions of a vacation somewhere, just the two of them where they could put aside their normal lives for a brief time.

"You will travel to Zulou, the capital of *Traisa*," she continued. "There, you will rendezvous with Supreme Autocrat Torray and convey him and his suite to Bharani Prime, an *Unaffiliated* world very close to *A'Zedi* space, where he will go into exile. The *Directorate* will provide for his planetary security on an ongoing basis."

Padraig understood that to mean a full military embargo of the planet, inspecting every vessel coming or going, regardless of the overall neutrality of the situation. And the players.

He would be walking on eggshells with this one, but nothing they hadn't done before.

He turned to his real boss.

"What pods?" he asked simply.

"A Courier for the Autocrat and an Escort-type Monitor Pod," Gelashvili replied in an even voice, which just about framed it perfectly for Padraig.

Courier made sense. He'd had a Starliner for Monsach, which was the double version and slightly upgraded, as a

Courier was for a diplomat or flag officer traveling with a smaller retinue.

Escort was in case a Tug like *Marrakesh* needed to sail into the line of battle replacing an Escort Cruiser. Wouldn't do as good a job, but it put a tremendous amount of shorter range firepower at his fingertips, suggesting that someone in the chain of command expected him to need it

Possibly an assassination attempt on Torray, but he couldn't be sure who might launch it. Might be *Traisa*. Might be *Wronlori*. Might even be something *A'Zedi* did if they needed deniability later.

He matched nods with Gelashvili as they both acknowledged things beyond their control.

"How soon?" he asked his boss.

"There should be tractors pulling them into place now," she replied.

At least his crew was sharp enough to understand that something was up. They'd be ready.

At least for that much of it.

2

———

Chance Messier was First Officer of *Marrakesh*, and occasionally still had to pinch herself that it wasn't a dream. It was certainly a dream job, because Padraig was about as good a captain and connection as she'd ever even heard of.

At some point, all that would serve her well in the rest of her career, whether she ended up commanding a ship somewhere or lateraled again back down into the depths of some of the things she'd done while grounded when Xandra and Daneel had been infants.

Today, shit had gone weird again. It did that pretty regularly around here, but she'd fortified with extra coffee and had the wardroom start a batch of scones for her, both sweet and savory, because she'd known what kind of day it was going to be as soon as a messenger had arrived in the middle of the night with Eyes-Only-Orders for Padraig.

And, because the crew had a pretty good idea, too, she'd gone ahead and signaled an alert—in dock and engines off— just to make sure everyone was on their toes.

"Commander, I have two tractors, approaching from

different directions, asking for rendezvous information," Nyssa Taggart said from her position at Radio.

Comms, Sensors, and Hyperadvanced Cryptographic Shenanigans.

Chance dialed on her comm.

"Stevedore," Kaitlin replied instantly. "This about the company coming to dinner?"

Trust Kaitlin Lynch to have reached out to old comrades from when she'd been doing this before retiring to become a highly-paid civilian contractor. Probably knew the pilots flying those tractors. And their bosses.

"Affirmative," Chance replied. "Got two."

"I'll take them and you can start on emergency resupply, Chance," Kaitlin offered.

"They're all yours," Chance said, cutting the line. "Taggart, route them to her and let me know what the station is rolling."

"Aye, sir," Nyssa said, then paused. "Sir, I've got a personnel transfer included in this batch. Your screen three."

By now, the fact that Nyssa could just take charge of Chance's controls from the Radio station no longer surprised Chance. She simply studied the record. Blinked when she recognized the name. Blinked again when she opened the file and recognized the face, too.

Knight Nafizul Haque.

Yeah, same guy. Quick scan of the bio confirmed that, including the two years where he'd been a field agent at the same time she'd been doing some really quiet and shadowy Analyst work in Naval Intelligence. At the time, Chance hadn't been sure there would be enough billets for bodies when she was ready for space again, so she'd gone wide and strange in pursuing certifications and working in any desk job someone needed a body.

A quick scan of the new file confirmed a connection she had previously suspected, but never asked because there were certain things you didn't bring up with folks who hadn't been in the business.

Still, she figured he should know.

Chance dialed a number aft.

"Electronics Shop. Haque."

Zadinul Haque. Expert Sailor in Engineering who specialized in exotic electronics and who had come quietly aboard after the *Northwind* mission, when Nyssa Taggart's console and tools had been radically upgraded by Intelligence Operations **again**. Zadi was the guy who fixed it when it broke, because even this crew didn't generally have the sorts of security clearances to know some of those things.

"It's Commander Messier," she said, grinning. "If you have a few minutes to spare, we'll be taking on a new crew member and I'd like you to get him aboard and situated, Haque."

Pause. Thinking. Possibly trying to gauge what she meant.

"Aye, sir," he replied. "How soon?"

"Your cousin Nafizul should be docking with the station then walking to the airlock in about six minutes," Chance said. "If you hurry, you can be there to welcome him."

Longer pause. Definite blip in his day.

"I'm on it, sir," he said, then cut the line.

Nyssa was looking back over a shoulder with some level of concern.

"Cousin?" she asked.

"I knew Nafizul from a previous posting," Chance nodded. "We worked together."

And leaving off the when or what was enough for Taggart to brighten up, then close right back down immediately and turn perfectly professional.

"Aye, sir," she said, then turned back to her station.

Chance kind of agreed on that.

Why the hell did *Marrakesh* need a former field agent and trained assassin as their new Gunnery Officer?

Where the hell was Intelligence sending them this time?

3

Nafizul was still a little uncertain about all this, but the surprise orders had been clear cut and extremely specific, giving him exactly enough time to dig his uniform out of the bag at the back of the closet and put it on, after making sure that he'd remembered to sew on the new rank of Knight.

He'd been in the field in civilian clothing for...long enough. And had previously only worn the damned thing for formal affairs and the like.

But that other part of his life was probably done.

He'd even managed to get out alive, and the limp was only evident when he was tired or had sat too long before standing up. The uniform would cover the scars, as long as he didn't ever go swimming.

Bag over his shoulder and order printout in one hand, Nafizul approached the airlock. Not a lot of chance that he could get the destination wrong, since the Agency had personally delivered him, but he was feeling a little at sea here.

But a year of rehab and retraining had supposedly prepared him to remain in harness somewhere.

A Tactical Transport? Hell of a comedown from what he'd been doing. At least a Gunnery Officer slot would take advantage of some of his skills, though there wasn't any windage or humidity to calculate in space.

A shadow appeared, just inside the open airlock. Two of them, but one was already stepping back as the other moved forward. Down the corridor, Nafizul could see forklifts and tractors loading large boxes into the cargo bays of the vessel, but his orders said to present himself here. Now.

Nafizul took a breath, held it, and stepped forward.

Then blinked.

"Zadi?" he asked.

"I'd ask if you'd gotten lost, but we already know the answer to that," his cousin teased.

Suddenly, he was twelve and that little shit had them turning the wrong way again and again as they got more lost, until they both got home so late that they'd been sent to bed without any supper. He'd never let the man hear the end of it after that, so he supposed some level of payback was appropriate here.

Nafizul grinned and felt a weight slide off his shoulders. He held up the papers and checked one last time.

"*Directorate* Cruiser, Tactical Transport *Marrakesh*?" he confirmed, reading the plaque next to the hatch and grinning at his grinning cousin. "Permission to come aboard?"

"Permission granted, Knight!" Zadi beamed. "Commander sent me down to get you aboard and taken care of, so let's try not to get lost on the way to the bridge, hey?"

Nafizul stepped over that bright blue line in the deck and was committed.

He simply had no idea to what.

4

Nyssa had checked with Commander Messier out of propriety, then been given clearance to read the same personnel file. The unredacted version, which was way more interesting and frankly a little frightening, all the more so because Nyssa understood some of those more cryptic code references that even most naval officers would miss.

Dude had literally killed people for a living. And with his bare hands. How had he managed to get assigned to *Marrakesh* to replace Misra?

Granted, Tanvi hadn't worked out. WAY too high strung for the sorts of missions they did. Maddox, without that calm certainty and the ability to dial it back at any moment.

Someone had called her a *murderhobo* at some point and it had stuck.

And now they had someone Commander Messier had known? Worked with in some of those places that Nyssa had been quietly read in on by other scary people?

None of the missions included names, but the assignment codes were all things she had memorized. Assassinations.

Destabilizations. Arson. Mayhem. Bank Robbery? Exfiltration?

Nyssa leaned back for a moment and took a deep breath, understanding suddenly that her life had been pretty simple, as things went. Electronic data to be sifted. Codes to be cracked for information to be gleamed out and distilled.

Nafizul Haque had gotten his hands dirty. Euphemistically, and that was about as far down that path as she wanted to go at the moment, even knowing that she had a career in Intelligence for as long as she wanted it, based on some of the comments sent her way.

There were whole other chunks of the business that she'd thought only existed in vids and books.

Apparently, those had some basis in reality.

One mission had gone as close to completely wrong as one man could still survive. Even with the euphemisms in the file, he should have been killed at least three times before they got him to safety and a long enough medical rehab that he was fit for duty on a warship.

Or at least a Transport Command vessel. Even this one.

Gunnery ratings as good as Tanvi and only a step below Maddox when he'd joined the ship, before Captain Boru had refined the man, as they both described it.

And retired spy. Or demobilized assassin. She wasn't sure what the term was. Might not be a term for it, because that man might have used up an entire lifetime of luck in those ninety-three minutes.

And gotten away.

Nyssa watched him interact with his cousin on a screen and noted the calmness overlying a fragility that might be more than just joining a new crew. Man had nearly died, and now he was back in the navy.

A chirp on her desk was a message from Captain Boru, in flight and returning. Confirming that there were no problems needing to be addressed.

Coded language, because everyone had known that a crash mission was landing on them. Wardroom had gone ahead and assumed extra coffee and put in an order for more from station stocks. And two tractors loading pods. And bodies in motion every which way.

"Loading in process for departure in ninety minutes," she replied, leaving off everything because he had to have just come from a briefing with the Secretary.

All Captain Boru needed to know was that they were handling things.

His happy face response put a smile on hers. One of these days, Captain Nyssa Taggart would be in the big chair, with everything she had learned from Boru, Messier, and a host of others.

She almost found herself looking forward to it.

5

———

Padraig had pulled Chance and Nyssa into his office with the new Gunner. Not exactly an inner circle sort of thing, but the people most specifically having direct Intelligence experience, instead of merely sailing on a ship with occasionally questionable missions.

"Knight Haque, welcome," he said to the man, studying the newcomer.

A'Zedi brown skin. Black hair kept short with some curls. Shoulders. Man had previously done a lot of bodybuilding work with iron, then transitioned to lean flexibility during rehab as he'd lost some ten kilos of mass.

Rather attractive face, but a little gunshy about a lot of things, per Secretary Gelashvili. Not cringing, but not smiling.

"You've met Commander Messier, my Second-In-Command, previously, from what I understand?" Padraig asked.

"In passing, sir," Haque replied. "Briefings and the like."

A nice way to finesse it. Padraig nodded.

"And you've been introduced to Squire Taggart," he continued, waiting for the man to turn and nod to Nyssa. "She has a Level Six Security Clearance, Mr. Haque. Mariami Gelashvili instructed me to tell you that up front. Chance and I are both generally at least Fives, as is your cousin. Most of the rest of the crew rate at least a Two, with the officers generally Three and above."

He paused and let the man digest that. Most ships might have a commanding officer with a Three. Maybe. Intelligence vessels like *Northwind* would run the other direction, and be much more like *Marrakesh*.

"I see, sir," Haque replied. "Good to know. As far as I have been informed, my current posting is merely naval."

"The extension of your rehabilitation from injuries sustained in the line of duty, yes," Padraig said, letting the man know that the three of them did understand more about him that just about anyone else would. "And your Gunnery scores are excellent, which was important here, because this vessel has seen more combat than most of the navy. My hope is that the current mission does not require a demonstration, but we are being loaded with a Monitor Pod Escort type, so I want you to spend time aft with Stevedore Lynch meeting the crew of the pod as well as getting to know the people in your department."

Padraig paused and studied the three of them.

"This is where things get interesting," he continued after they nodded. "We will be picking up a small diplomatic team and carrying them to *Traisa*."

Chance's face scrunched.

"Why would they need us or this much firepower for something so mundane as that, Padraig?" she asked.

"Because when we get there, Supreme Autocrat Torray intends to step down and go into exile, transported to an

Unaffiliated world aboard this vessel," he said, watching that impact their minds. "That does not leave this office."

Blinks. He understood that. It was insane on the surface of things. At the same time, *Marrakesh* might be the perfect vessel to deploy for such an operation, because the *A'Zedi Navy* didn't build Diplomatic cruisers. Why bother, when you had Couriers and Starliners that could be used in those few circumstances when it came up?

And normally, *Marrakesh* only had frigate firepower on a cruiser hull, but that Escort pod gave them a mass of extra particle cannons, six arranged in a single line down the center with the outer two singles and the inner two twin batteries, plus a tremendous amount of excess generator power to fire them and do everything else in battle.

"Will there be other vessels involved?" Chance asked.

"I don't know," Padraig replied. "No *A'Zedi* warships, because *Traisa* is neutral, but we're technically a cargo hauler so we aren't immediately seen as a threat. As you might expect, the situation will remain fluid until the moment things crystallize. We'll be stopping midway there to pick up a Division Marshal with Ambassadorial credentials, hauling him to *Traisa* as part of the cover, then he will be Torray's point of contact on the next leg."

"Point of contact?" Nyssa asked, a touch confused.

"A legalistic fig leaf for the man who will become Torray's jailer, Radio," Padraig explained, watching her absorb that and nod. "He gets to leave *Traisa* alive, but once we deliver him, he's never leaving that world again."

Padraig had asked the questions Nyssa refrained from now, because it would be his ship and his ass on the line, so the Director had explained it.

They were helping the man escape with his life, but then they were making sure he stayed retired.

Permanently, though Padraig didn't think that Haque would be using his other skills on this mission.

At least he hoped not.

6

———————

Tom Ussher studied the officers arranged to meet him as he came aboard the Tactical Transport *Marrakesh*, supposedly last of the M-boats still in service. The fleet was moving to P-boats soon for their cruisers, so this vessel was probably as old as he was.

Well, at least he would have a full courier pod to himself and his staff. Those were always kept to the best standards.

"Division Marshal, I am Captain Padraig Boru," the closest man introduced himself. "Welcome aboard. This is Commander Messier, my First Officer. Stevedore Lynch here will see to your personal staff aboard the pod and be your point of contact in towards the crew, but do not hesitate to reach out to me directly if you have issues. We've been briefed on the delicate nature of the mission and look forward to how we might serve your peculiar needs to see this mission successful."

Tom paused and absorbed that. Boru was young. Tom had been concerned, but he'd read a partially-redacted file indicating that the man and his crew were far more than they seemed. And exceptionally competent. Enough so for the man to have been promoted from Knight almost directly to Captain to take command of this vessel, after which he had been moved...*elsewhere.*

"I look forward to the trip, Captain Boru. Stevedore Lynch," Tom said properly, noting that the rest of the officers and crew handy all had a calm surety as they watched him.

No fidgeting. No noise. Nothing but professional faces looking back.

He turned to indicate the woman trailing him.

"Captain Yasmin Moneaux, my Chief of Staff," Tom introduced her.

"Would you prefer a quick tour of the vessel, or should we see you to your pod, Marshal?" Boru asked.

Tom found himself impressed. Often, young hotshots like this were at pains to make themselves visible to senior officers. To be busybodies. Boru was utterly professional in his demeanor, but Tom had been warned by certain folks that *Marrakesh* and it's crew were far more than they seemed.

Hopefully, for the better.

"A quick tour, I think," Tom replied. "We can get underway from the bridge. Time is not critical, but it will factor."

"Excellent, sir," Boru replied. "And, as an aside, we have been known to reach Mark Six and better on the Ghostdrives, if speed becomes an issue."

Tom blinked before he could catch himself. An old tub like this should be lucky to hit Mark Five on a good day.

Yes, obviously more than they seemed.

What other surprises awaited?

"Lead on, Captain," Tom ordered, following the man into his vessel.

7

Padraig might have been warned by Madam Gelashvili that Division Marshal Ussher was a bit of stickler for things, so he'd had everyone spend the last two days cleaning. Squire Zarah Halloran had the bridge when he arrived, and had specifically moved from her station to his, though normally whichever officer was in command remained where they were most comfortable.

In an emergency, that saved five to ten seconds of bodies having to rearrange themselves when things might be critical.

Still, she rose when he entered.

"Marshal on the bridge," she called.

Regulations did not require the crew to stand and come to attention while on active duty, even in dock like this, but everyone looked up and acknowledged the man before returning to their screens.

Ussher swept in behind him and looked around.

"Boru, how soon were you intending to depart?" the man asked.

"We took aboard a resupply container immediately on arrival, sir," Padraig replied. "We could depart now, if you would prefer to give the order yourself."

That surprised him, but Madam Secretary was a wily and dangerous boss. She and the Director had been expecting the need to impress this man, and had provided Padraig the tools.

Ussher looked at him hard, but Padraig projected *helpful*, understanding the men like Tom Ussher didn't get to do this anymore. They commanded squadrons and sectors, not cruisers.

Forewarned is forearmed. Ussher relented and turned to Zarah.

"You have the deck, Squire?" he asked in a formal voice.

"Aye, sir," she replied crisply.

Padraig glanced over and confirmed that Doolan Ennis was sitting Helm at the moment. Expert sailor. Quiet and a little nerdy most of the time.

Calm.

"Helm, is there a course laid in?" Ussher asked the back of Ennis's head.

"Aye, sir."

Because again, Padraig had impressed on everyone the need to be two steps or more ahead of their passenger today.

Ussher even smiled. It was gone like a ghost, but Padraig noted it.

"Helm, undock from the station," Division Marshal Ussher ordered.

"All hands, stand by to undock," Ennis announced on the intercom.

Zarah took the Captain's chair again and buckled herself in.

Ten seconds passed, then Ennis pressed a button on his screen.

Aft, the first of a series of rapid chunks as locks opened in sequence, stern to bow.

"Vessel is flying free, sir."

Normally, Padraig simply gave the order to get underway and let Zarah and her people handle it, but he'd warned everyone to study the book for one. Ennis waited, poised but not going ahead without a specific order.

Ussher might have waited a tad longer than one would expect.

"Helm, engage rotary thrusters," Ussher called. "Ten percent power until you have cleared the dock."

"Ahead ten on plane, aye."

By the book. Ussher nodded to himself.

"Marshal, we have cleared all navigation hazards," Ennis announced after two minutes of utter silence broken only by life support blowers and beeps on consoles.

Again, waiting. Poised. Professional.

"Helm, time to Ghostdrives?" the Marshal asked.

"Stand by, sir," Ennis replied. "Engineering, what is your status?"

"All generators online and warm, Bridge," Jareth Ahearn answered. "Ready as you bear."

Ennis nodded and cut the line.

"All systems ready, Marshal."

Padraig allowed himself a smile as well. Brief and internal, but there.

"Helm, take us out," Ussher called, finally sounding friendly.

He turned to Padraig and nodded, conveying a wealth of approvals.

"Well run ship, Boru. Let's go see about that Courier Pod."

Padraig nodded and gestured Kaitlin to lead them to her realm.

8

———————

Kaitlin's job was usually an even mix of Loadmaster and Den Mother. Here, she'd spent the last week wearing three hats, but that was because the new Gunner was also needing her assistance with the gun teams that had arrived with the Escort pod, at the same time she was dealing with a flag officer.

She'd done her thirty years and retired. As a civilian, she was making about three times the salary for basically the same job. And wasn't in anybody's chain of command.

The Division Marshal had discovered quickly enough that she would simply smile at him, then outwait the man. His staff must have said something, because he'd relaxed some around her.

Not old drinking buddies, but not white-gloving her mission pods that had come aboard from storage for this trip, either.

Meals with him and Captain Moneaux had gotten more pleasant. Padraig and Chance had even hosted him with the officers on the main hull last night with great success.

She still preferred runs where the pods were cargo carriers instead.

But she smiled as they completed lunch. The Courier Pod came with a professional staff who either cooked for whatever base they were assigned to, or the crew and passengers when the pod was deployed. Top rate cooks, too, used to fussy berks, though Ussher was simply precise about things.

"And you returned to duty in spite of retiring, Lynch?" Ussher asked as the plates got removed by silent and efficient stewards.

"I was hired back as a civilian contractor, Marshal," she corrected him lightly. Again. "Since then, I've had a marvelous time working with Captain Boru and his team."

Because when Padraig got promoted, she was likely leaving again. Even Chance wouldn't be as much fun. And anybody else would be a demotion as far as she saw it.

But Fleet had understood that and bent over backwards to keep folks together, though Maddox was off having adventures now with Survey Command.

"And your previous missions?" he pressed. "Were they all so interesting?"

"As I'm sure you've been briefed, Marshal, *Marrakesh* occasionally serves other masters," she smiled. Technically, the *other master* these days was Transport Command, with Padraig being fully immersed in Intelligence Operations by now. But they all knew that. "The crew will handle this one with similar precision."

The upgunning did give her pause, but Kaitlin hoped that it was someone being extra prepared rather than knowing something they hadn't mentioned.

A'Zedi and *Traisa* were friendly on the surface, but not allied at present. A new Supreme Autocrat shortly—and she had no doubts that things would get tense when the truth came out—was likely to realign things, though she didn't know enough to guess if they grew closer or hostile afterwards.

"On Monsach, I note that the ship's Gunner had to get involved with a planetside combat operation on an *Unaffiliated* world?" Ussher offered, leadingly.

"We went to great lengths to keep things under control when they threatened to spill out in a damaging way, sir," she offered blandly. "That Gunner has since been promoted to his own command. The new gentleman has a good background in such operations, as well as top notch ratings in Gunnery command. All in all, a ship and crew exceptionally competent at doing all the little things quietly."

"I've noted that," Ussher told her. "At what point might outsiders come to understand what this ship really does? And who it does it for?"

Kaitlin paused before she answered. The stewards all had to be highly screened, considering who they served regularly, but they were still outsiders. Thus, the man had spoken somewhat obliquely, while still centering on a specific point. And waited until the three of them were alone.

"There may be folks out there with suspicions, but Captain Boru had always gone to careful lengths to disguise certain things, Marshal," she replied. "Opposition forces might have files, but such things are likely still more supposition than common knowledge. Especially as Fleet has taken great pains keeping things quieter than one might suspect with many of our more important missions."

He nodded. Smiled in a wry, knowing way that showed her how attractive he was, then turned serious again.

"So if we end up having to fight our way out of this one on

the far side, one way or the other, you have confidence?" he asked.

Kaitlin confirmed that they were still alone. Three of them, with Captain Moneaux having gone perfectly silent for several minutes. Watching. Recording. Not commenting.

"I have not seen our new Gunner in action yet, sir," she offered blandly. "But Captain Boru is rather expert at fighting a warship himself if it becomes necessary, that being his previous vocation. As for the departure, it is my hope that everyone kisses us on both cheeks and waves as we go."

She saw the doubt in the man's eyes, there and gone, but Padraig had also taken her aside and shared a few things he had learned.

Jailer for a soon-to-be-former Supreme Autocrat. At least for a time. Until things settled enough that you didn't need one of the senior officers in the fleet immediately on call to issue orders or override even squadron commanders.

"Is Boru's luck that good?" Ussher asked her, point blank.

"He manufactures his luck, Marshal," Kaitlin countered. "As does the rest of this crew. If you need them to step into the breach, they'll be there for you."

That mollified him, but Kaitlin also saw the hard edges to the man. Quite possibly dropped into an impossible situation, though the right people had put Padraig in his corner.

And *Marrakesh*.

9

—————

Padraig had rotated watch schedules around, once they had hit *Traisan* space and started inwards to the capital at Zulou.

A *Traisan* Super-Cruiser had met them at the border when they'd arrived. Heavier than an *A'Zedi* cruiser but lighter than a Ship of the Line. Supposedly all the speed of the former and all the guns of the latter, but those folks had also been at pains to be polite when he called on them.

Not friendly, but they'd obviously been ordered to behave by their Supreme Autocrat, and had no reason to question that.

One did not question the Supreme Autocrat.

"Mr. Haque, what's our new friend up to?" Padraig asked.

After two weeks, the newcomer had settled some. Significantly older than Nyssa or Zarah, almost Chance's age and just a little younger than Padraig, but he'd had a long detour out of line command positions between.

"Still maintaining a position on our rear flank, Captain," Haque replied. "Just under fifteen seconds behind us at Mark Four, one hundred and fifty degrees true."

Padraig nodded at that. A hound, tracking a fox but not pouncing yet. Making sure that *Marrakesh* didn't veer off or do anything that compromised their status as a diplomatic transport hauling Ussher to Zulou.

Because there were very few people inside the *Enlightened Tyranny of Traisa* that knew the truth. Padraig occasionally wondered if Torray had handled the Aetherial Communications Array himself when sending the message. Or had at least personally coded and decoded the transmissions.

The risk was exceptionally high that someone else might understand what was going on and simply assassinate the man to handle the situation. *Traisa* didn't have elections for their executive positions, after all.

Well, one man or woman would elect themselves, in a neck-or-crown kind of campaign.

And *Marrakesh* was about to sail right into the center of it.

"Helm, how long to arrival?" Padraig asked, mostly to keep people on their toes.

He could look up Zarah's running calculations himself, after all.

"Seventeen minutes, Captain," she replied without looking up.

Under a light-year, because they would slow as they got close, then drop out right under the guns of several major orbital platforms and a fleet or two.

Fortunately, he had an invitation.

Padraig dialed a number aft.

"Courier Pod. Moneaux."

"This is Captain Boru," he told the woman, presuming that Ussher and Kaitlin were in the same room at this point. "Roughly fifteen minutes to arrival, if anyone would care to witness from the bridge."

Not normally something he preferred, but Padraig would just as soon Ussher be the one on the spot, considering the implications here.

"Noted, Captain Boru," she said. "We will join you shortly."

The line cut and he looked around. Everything cleaned up still and everyone nodding, having heard and understood that a flag officer would be looking over their shoulders shortly.

10

Tom stood to one side of Boru's station as *Marrakesh* dropped out of Ghost-space.

As expected, they were challenged immediately by a pair of Heavy Annihilators in close orbit. Vessels able to defeat an *A'Zedi* Ship of the Line, one on one. Generally defensive because the design was a bulldog that was all teeth, with horrible sailing characteristics over any decent range.

Cramped and smelly, according to reports from some of the spies who had seen such designs from the inside. He smiled as the painfully-young Radio Officer, Squire Taggart, handled the other ships with much greater aplomb and maturity than he would have expected from a sailor directly commissioned out of ground school.

But then, the whole ship had impressed him with how good they were. It gave him hope that he could pull this one off, when he'd told the folks on Horwin that he rated his chances of success at roughly one in five. And that if everything broke his way.

After two weeks with Boru's people, Tom was willing to

bump that to one in three. But only one chance in three of succeeding.

Too many moving pieces, like juggling knives. That were on fire. Blindfolded.

Taggart cut the line and looked pointedly back to both him and Boru.

"We're cleared to take up a geosynchronous orbital position that puts us directly over the city of Jensen itself and under the guns of two stations and presumably at least one full battle squadron, sirs," she offered without any emotion beyond conveying information.

Boru glanced over. Tom nodded.

"Helm, take us in," Boru ordered. "Radio, refrain from any active scanning while we are in port, but I believe that having your team collect as much passive information as we can while we're here would not be a bad idea."

Tom nodded to that, too. Delicate. Finesse. *Marrakesh* was a spy ship. And had been upgraded more than Tom had originally expected, including this crew. Their standards for data were probably equally high.

He wasn't sure what anyone would do with it. Then he corrected himself.

Whoever replaced Torray might decide to be angry at *A'Zedi* for getting involved. Might even shift over to the *Wronlori* side of things. Maybe the War of the Fifth Alliance would evolve out of the Fourth.

His job then, to make sure that didn't happen. And to prepare Command if it did.

"Radio, contact the palace and transmit them my credentials," he ordered Taggart, mostly to save the kabuki of ordering Boru to order it. This crew didn't strike him for the need to have someone holding their hand, every step of the way.

Tom turned to an expectant Captain Boru.

"Given the fluidity of things at this point, you should be prepared for an invitation to visit the palace, Captain," Tom told the man.

"What are you orders when it arrives, Marshal?"

Tom grinned.

"Polite, friendly, and neutral, as if this were another *Unaffiliated* world, Captain," Tom told him. "While your people keep as low a profile as possible and are ready to run like hell if they have to."

"Sir, on our best day, *Marrakesh* could not outrun that Super-Cruiser," the Gunner spoke up. Again, no emotions beyond providing a superior officer information with which to make better decisions. "Nor could we outfight them."

Tom agreed. Even with the record this crew had accumulated, some things were simply impossible.

"Noted, Haque," Tom replied. "See what scenarios you might prepare for, if we did have to make a break for it. Necessary fallbacks, because this is an accredited diplomatic mission. At least for now."

"Should we assume ground leave, sir?" Boru asked carefully.

"Let me take the temperature of the palace, Captain," Tom replied.

Boru nodded succinctly and Tom settled back as the ship settled into the center of a spotlight.

He would have to bring his own cloak to shadow things.

Or manufacture it.

11

———

Nyssa had already programmed her machines to drink in as much data as they could flow inwards, knowing that an entire cabin aft had been converted to a monumentally huge bucket of extra datastores to hold it.

A'Zedi spy ships simply never got invited anyplace interesting, but they were Marshal Ussher's transport, and the Supreme Autocrat wasn't in a position to throw a fit.

Not if he wanted them to carry him away later.

So she dialed in every optical telescope with a gyroscope. Every passive sensor got aimed at anything interesting she could find.

And someone had provided her with both an up-to-date set of diplomatic code books, as well as a few guesses about how *Traisan* code machines were programmed. Pure hypothesis, but a good starting point.

Captain Boru and the Marshal had departed. Technically, Knight Haque was in command with Messier off duty at the moment, but she and Zarah had quietly agreed that he wasn't fully prepared for that sort of thing. Not yet. Maddox had been, but he'd come from a Line Cruiser. Nafizul had had... other jobs prior to this.

So she and Zarah had both rotated their departments so they could pull longer shifts today, just in case.

The bridge was quiet, but that was them sailing carefully in a pre-defined orbit that kept them where the locals wanted them. Just in case.

"Radio, how good are your systems?" Nafizul inquired after a time. "The amount and crispness of the data I'm reviewing here seems at odds with what I remember from other bridges."

He left it at that. Man had shifted to Captain's station, but that was a Marshal aboard. Chief Tindal had shifted herself from Secondary Bridge forward to handle guns. Again, experts on duty when you had strangers around and aboard.

"Top notch, sir," she replied, turning to look at him specifically. "The sorts of things you would have expected, providing you the depth and breadth necessary for certain missions."

He blinked. Caught on. Nodded.

Man was smart. Just wasn't used to the uniform. Probably only wore it for Fleet Day when he was somewhere appropriate. And from what she'd seen, than hadn't happened often.

"Taggart, what can you tell me specifically about the vessel *Crimson Firebird*?" he asked after a pause. "That Super-Cruiser that trailed us in."

"The design has been accused of fragility, sir," Nyssa replied, rotating to open up a section of her secured files that most people didn't get a chance to read. Like, ever. "Sacrifices were made by taking an Annihilator hull and trading weight of armor and interior bracing for more missiles and tubes, plus generators for excessive numbers of guns, among the highest count of any vessel in my database."

"If trouble breaks out, I presume that they'll be the one to worry, then," Haque announced. "We can outrun most of them and outshoot the rest. Taggart, I would greatly appreciate it if you spent a little extra time on that class, since I see two in orbit from your records. Find me his limits in combat?"

Nyssa processed that and appreciated that the man was being polite and respectful. Probably because the others treated her that way, in spite of usually outranking her. Zarah was the only one below her on seniority, technically.

"Aye, sir," she replied crisply.

She was already doing that, but it was good that he'd looked at everything around them and started a stack rank against trouble.

Like a Gunner was supposed to do.

12

———

Padraig had accompanied Ussher to the ground on invite from the palace. Normal stuff in a diplomatic situation. Even here.

Everything by a different book than he was used to, but *Marrakesh* had carried diplomats hither and yon as part of other missions, so he'd lived through it.

Just never at these stakes.

Diplomatic reception, which usually involved important politicians inviting wealthy locals and acknowledged spies to stand around and chat. Open bar and finger foods. Wait staff in black. Where espionage sometimes took on a more genteel quality, but a safer one, because messages could be delivered quietly, rather than blasting one another in the media or yelling insults across a conference table while pounding a fist.

He found himself standing around in one of his better uniforms while talking to a local woman in a gown that was mostly backless, largely frontless, and possibly enough to get arrested for indecency in a few places. He'd seen women in swimming suits with more fabric.

Or maybe she was just getting on his nerves with her barely-subtle innuendo and general flirtiness.

He supposed that she was attractive enough, but he could see signs of plastic surgery here and there that added at least a decade to her supposed coquettish giggle. Rough, hard years, too. Hair had been touched up, but she needed a better stylist who could do a more professional than just bringing everything to a universal blonde.

Or maybe she should had done her eyebrows, too.

Considering the location and the crowd, he wondered which organization was attempting to seduce him. And if they were incompetent or merely clueless.

It wasn't that he didn't like women. In small doses and odd occasions. They just didn't generally do that much for him. At least until they opened their mouths and had something interesting to say.

This one probably didn't even know how to spell vapid. But he smiled. Nodded. Answered the occasional question with something more than one-syllable words, while not addressing anything nor admitting it.

Noise and movement on his right caused Padraig to rotate. Not ignoring the woman, but ignoring her. Anything to get away from another hint about a quickie in the cloak room.

Noise had surged, then collapsed, like a wave hitting the shore.

"And this is Captain Padraig Boru," Marshal Ussher was introducing him to...

The Supreme Autocrat was a short man in person. At least on first appearance. Padraig was a shade above average at 186cm. Arodd Torray was as much below, running perhaps 175. Padraig was, however, somewhat leanly built, while the

Autocrat gave the impression of a bulldog, much like those ships in orbit.

Shoulders right on the verge of hulking. Thick neck. Traps that should have their own mailing code. Arms like Padraig's legs and legs like tree trunks. At the same time, the man had a flat stomach and none of the bureaucratic sprawl in his ass that a lot of them got. Wasn't a runner. Not with that physique. Horseman, maybe. He gave off vibes of a knight just off horseback who had stripped off the steel armor. Or the kind of man who threw trees around as a sport.

Padraig bowed his head.

"Supreme Autocrat," he said in a quiet tone as the mob of folks with Torray engulfed him. At least the bimbo had gotten politely shoved out of the picture. He'd have to ask later who she worked for that she'd gotten an invitation.

"*Marrakesh* is a Tactical Transport, Captain?" Torray asked pointedly.

"Aye, sir," Padraig replied.

"What pods are you currently running?" the man asked, as though he couldn't have gotten that information from his own fleet people.

Padraig presumed a test.

"Courier for the Ambassador, plus an Escort pod because we were crossing uncertain regions of space and could not be certain of our reception," he told the man.

"Not a combat module, Captain?" Torray pressed.

Ussher had slipped just enough out of the picture to make this a conversation between the two of them. Putting Padraig on the spot, but in front of all the witnesses.

"We're an Ambassadorial mission, Supreme Autocrat," Padraig reminded the man. "Combat with *Traisan* forces was literally at the bottom of the list of concerns. It was the potential for pirates and privateers outside the *Enlightened Tyranny of Traisa* that set the standards for things."

Torray watched him for a long moment, then smiled. Ussher relaxed a shade.

"Excellent, Boru," Torray replied. "I look forward taking a tour of your vessel and seeing how the *Directorate* does things. My staff will contact yours before you depart."

Padraig bowed more fully to the man, recognizing a dismissal for what it was as Torray turned to a woman in his group and nodded her to stay put, even as the rest continued circling the room, Ussher and Moneaux at the center of things.

Padraig paused to consider all the subtle messages that had just been conveyed.

Then he addressed himself to the woman left behind.

13

Padraig found it unfortunate that she immediately followed the bimbo in conversation, as she was literally at the other end of just about any spectrum you might wish to compare them.

Short. Muscular like her boss, but not as nearly defined. Padraig wondered if the weight room and the athletic field were the places advisors had to go—and shine—if they wished to get ahead around here.

Short hair in a stylish pixie cut just a little less brown than Padraig's. Dark blue eyes, much more common in *Traisa*. Brains obvious.

He wondered if she was Torray's spy or his current jailer. Ussher had suggested that ultimate power in *Traisa* was as much a prison as it was a reward, hemmed in on all sides by people who resented that power and were constantly maneuvering to get more for themselves. Or take it from someone else.

The bimbo had vanished. *Good riddance* was rude, but essentially accurate.

The woman sized him up.

"Equerry Irelyn Cayne," she said, emphasizing the title.

Equerry was an office of honor. Historically, a senior household attendant with responsibilities for the stables of a monarch, though in contemporary use more like an aide-de-camp. Someone Torray trusted to get things done, though Padraig had no hints as to who she did them for. Or to.

"Captain Padraig Boru," he replied. "Commanding officer, *Marrakesh*. How may I be of service?"

Because that was his job around here. Make Ussher look good and backstop the man to pull off one of the most audacious stunts Padraig could remember.

He waited, pasting something of his own vapid smile on, just in case it might fool any of these people. He doubted it, but anything was possible.

"How long were your orders to remain on station?" she asked, betraying a solid naval background with her vocabulary.

Or one hell of a good briefing by someone who knew their shit.

"Until Division Marshal Ussher was credentialed by your government properly," Padraig replied, just as crisp. He'd also been briefed by some scary people. "The expectation was up to three weeks, with a need to resupply if we were to stay past that."

"And then?" Hard eyes. Hard mouth. Hard woman.

Not as physically attractive as he supposed the bimbo was, but Padraig had different standards. No one around here had looked closely at him, obviously.

"I have some cargo to deliver to Bharani Prime," he finessed her, mostly watching her eyes for a hint as to how much she knew. "On my way home to base."

Unaffiliated worlds located close to *A'Zedi* borders shouldn't mean anything to the woman.

Unless they did.

Those eyes gave nothing away.

"The Autocrat expects a tour of your vessel," she repeated unnecessarily. "I will need to come aboard and clear things ahead of time. How soon can you be prepared?"

Considering Ussher's standards, Padraig simply smiled at the woman.

"My intention was to return to the ship either tonight after dinner, or first thing in the morning, depending on circumstances," he said. "How much prep will you need?"

Caught her off guard. He actually saw emotion in those eyes for the briefest flash. Surprise. It was gone just as quickly. Back to normal and hard.

He waited.

If the Equerry was an outsider, she didn't need to know anything useful, other than *Marrakesh* was cleaned up for an extremely precise flag officer to travel aboard. Maybe a step beyond what Padraig normally maintained, but he had also never been that commander who put on the white gloves and went looking for ways to punish and demean his crews.

Not if they got the job done to his standards, which were often lower than theirs to his ongoing delight.

If she was an insider, they could talk when she came aboard, safe from eavesdropping ears.

Not a lot to say until that point.

Beyond calling her bluff.

Padraig waited. Watched. Breathed.

As a former commanding officer had liked to drawl, "This ain't my first rodeo."

"We will return to your vessel tonight, Captain," she abruptly decided.

He bowed but he was already looking at her back.

Didn't offend him.

He was here to do a job.

Politics around here wouldn't be nearly as risky as what was coming.

14

Nyssa got the message, routed from System Control as part of a package of other messages being sent.

Every ship that arrived anywhere usually got cold-called by local vendors. Bumboats to sell the crew fresh fruit or trinkets or companionship. Coupons for brothels and museums on the ground, all drumming up business.

The *Enlightened Tyranny of Traisa* might be screwed down a little tighter on morality issues than the *Directorate* tended to be, but sailors were sailors, so she ignored most of it.

This particular message had a code embedded that triggered a whole raft of secondary flags and got shunted off to her because it was from the Captain and included a word from a list the two of them had worked up. Nothing anyone could guess, and not something he would tell anyone.

** Returning after early dinner. Household Equerry accompanying. **

Nyssa wondered if he'd gotten lucky, then looked up the Equerry and presumed not. First off, she was a woman. Second, she looked like a spy. Something in the eyes, because spies tended to be introverts and politicians were always trying to either fuck you through the camera or sell you something.

Since she had a public data connection to the local network, Nyssa looked up Irelyn Cayne and read as much bio as the Autocrat's household allowed. Not a lot.

No mention of spouse or family. She paused and looked up a few others who did list such things, so presumably unattached. Nyssa wondered if the woman was Torray's lover, as he was divorced from two women, with three known children, all under sixteen and not associated with the Household.

Quality educational background. Household politics flags Nyssa had identified from others.

Insider, though true outsiders like Nyssa didn't have much visibility into *Traisan* politics at the very top. Cut-throat only began to describe it. If she really needed to know more, Nyssa could ask Knight Haque, as he'd been on missions to *Traisa*, though none recently.

Still, important news.

"Flight deck. Rafferty."

"Air Boss, it's Taggart," she said. "Captain and guest arriving in roughly five hours. We'll need a spare officer's cabin, but I'll talk to Kaitlin and have her coordinate with you."

"Deck's clean, Radio," he said, a smile in his voice. "Cap warned us about surprise inspections."

"This feels like one," she told him.

"We're ready here."

She cut the line.

"Stevedore."

"It's Nyssa," she replied. "I have the watch. Could you join me in the Captain's day office? I have some questions."

Pause as Kaitlin absorbed that.

"I'll be right along," the woman replied, then cut the line.

Nyssa wasn't sure what to expect, but that might be being the youngest officer aboard. And maybe a little sheltered before now, which she would blame on realizing all the *other things* Intelligence Operations did, wrapped up in the form of Nafizul Haque.

It was kinda scary out there. Good thing she had folks like him around.

15

———

Kaitlin slid into a chair in Padraig's office, noting that Nyssa seemed a bit...off.

"Spill," she said, which she could do because honestly Nyssa was not *quite* young enough to be a grandchild.

"Captain Boru will be returning to the ship tonight, as expected," Nyssa began. "The Household Equerry, a woman named Irelyn Cayne, will be accompanying him. I don't think we should read too much into that."

Kaitlin grinned. Sailors didn't often form good marriages because they were gone so much. And so long. She'd had her adventures, but gotten a little bored being home and jumped at this gig when they called her out of the blue. Didn't have any boyfriends or girlfriends pining away anywhere.

At least as far as she knew.

"We'll assume she's a spy," Kaitlin stated simply. "The question is whose. Or rather, how many people she might be reporting to. Seems quick on their part to put someone aboard, so you might have Zadi meander around with one of his scanners and make sure she's not up to anything while she is here."

Nyssa's eyes lit up on that one, so Kaitlin nodded.

"How can I assist you, Radio?" she asked.

Nyssa thought about it for a moment.

"Would he and his people move this quickly?" she asked.

Kaitlin considered her response.

"They might, if they felt the walls suddenly closing in on them," she replied. "Much could have happened while we were inbound. Or someone suspected the reason for our visit. Alternatively, someone else might have wondered if they could do the same thing, not realizing they were echoing their boss. Why the concern?"

"Captain's message had a code work signaling potential trouble, but not what," Nyssa offered.

"He might not know," Kaitlin said. "Remember, for all that we've spent a few weeks preparing for this, he and Tom Ussher only just landed and got introduced to all the main players locally. I would expect a variety of maneuvers to see what's what."

"She likely to be surprised, if she has other ulterior motives?" Nyssa asked.

Kaitlin grinned at her.

"He's not entirely opposed to women," she reminded Nyssa. "Jocelyn Konicek from the *Northwind* mission, though she was an exceptional example. This is likely just a spy, doing spy things. We should keep a lower profile than one might expect though. At least until we know whose side she is on. Any hints?"

"None," Nyssa grumbled. "And I doubt that she'll come out and tell us."

"Do we need to seduce her?" Kaitlin asked. "Padraig might carry through, but I doubt that his heart would be in it."

"Nafizul has operational experience, according to his records."

"Does he now?" Kaitlin asked.

She had remained generally on the fringe of things, but Padraig and Chance had both mentioned tidbits.

Nyssa, however, had turned dark umber with blush.

"Uhm, yeah?" she muttered.

Kaitlin supposed that she might have had a lifetime more experience than the rather shy and reserved Radio. At least at certain things.

"If you feel it necessary, I'd be happy to talk to him and Padraig on the topic," she offered, watching Nyssa relax some.

Kaitlin could only imagine how that conversation might have gone. Nyssa probably passing out from embarrassment and the two men even more confused.

"Thank you," Nyssa said, recovering some. "Also, if she is coming aboard, I presume that we need to at least prepare a cabin for her to stay in tonight, regardless of whether she uses it or not?"

And the blush was back. Bad.

Kaitlin refrained from teasing her, but could see possibly hauling the youngster ashore at some point for a girl's weekend. Possibly get her a little drunk and find some cute boytoys to throw at her to loosen her up some. Or at least give her more experience with the topic for later.

"Tom has been using the Chief of Staff cabin in the Pod," Kaitlin told her. "Yasmin has been in another spare, so we could put her right into the Ambassador's space. Have Zadi scan the shit out of her coming and going, then have housekeeping strip it to the walls and clean it within an inch of its life after she leaves."

"Do you think that's necessary?" Nyssa asked.

"Would you rather take that chance?" Kaitlin countered.

They shared a nod.

Best to go overboard. Just in case.

16

Zadinul had generally not hassled his cousin all that much. Enlisted men didn't sass officers on the ship. That could wait for shore leave.

And they were in different departments, with Nyssa Taggart as Zadi's boss. Scary smart woman.

He listened to her finish her explanation.

"Sure, boss," Zadi said. "I could build you something. Might just take the Quasiprobe from a Resonant Thermometer and crosswire a couple of electronics sniffers in. What am I looking for?"

"I want you to hard scan everything as it exists right now, then again when she leaves," Radio ordered. "At a level of detail where we can go through the logs manually against false positives later, in case she leaves anything. Also, you will be handy when she boards, and I want her sheep-dipped. Hard."

Zadi nodded. Technically a veterinary term, but espionage had adopted it. You dipped sheep to kill bugs and things.

"Main personnel airlock from the flight deck, sir?" he asked.

"What do you need to happen?" she countered.

At least she understood that enlisted folks occasionally had good ideas. He occasionally had bad ones, too, but navigation software existed for a reason.

"I can build something," Zadi told her. "Install it on the hatch and have everyone walk through individually, coming and going. That baselines us both directions and provides sanitized individuals as well."

He watched her check the time.

"You have ninety minutes to get it built and installed, whatever it is," she said simply. "Grab anybody you need for welding and wiring, including me. We're on the clock."

Zadi nodded, pausing to shape a few things in his head. Most of it already existed, because he had a great boss who expected some level of tinkering in a secured room, so he had stuff he could adapt pretty quickly.

Now he just had to make it work.

17

Nafizul had allowed himself exactly one second of sourness when the Stevedore explained her idea to him and the Exec. At least the woman in the picture wasn't ugly.

Still, he'd thought that he'd put that portion of his career behind him. *Rehabbed* and *Resurrected*, as it were.

"And, mind you," Lynch continued, "this is entirely supposition on my part, extrapolating random clues from chaotic noise and attempting to backstop the situation at its weirdest. None of it has any grounding in reality, but this is one of those moments when things need to be assessed ahead of time so we are prepared. Haque, you will make the ultimate call."

He nodded at that. Both women were older than him. Slightly and a generation respectively, but Messier had done formal intelligence work before *Marrakesh* and the others were exceptionally gifted amateurs from his first month among them.

He could have done so much worse in the second half of his career.

"Given the lateness of the day and them embarking almost immediately after a formal dinner, I presume a quick reception for the woman, then someone putting her to bed in the Pod," Nafizul replied, bringing his operational expertise to the fore. Both women nodded. "Lynch, that's your task. Command crew on day shift sort of thing. Lock the pod itself when you all are inside, then have Security put a camera on the hatch, but not a guard."

"Passive perimeter in layered rings," Lynch nodded. "Got it."

He turned the Executive Officer. Desk-bound Analyst, then and now, but really smart. And a breadth of life experience that most of them never got, which he appreciated a lot better today than he had at twenty-three. "Am I throwing myself at her, or being available? And why not the Captain handling this?"

Messier had a sly smile he would have expected on a much older woman. The other one in this office.

"For One, Captain Boru rates about a ten percent on a heterosexuality scale, Haque," she said clinically. "Not opposed to women, but hardly interested unless they're exceptional. Two, this lets them compromise you without going after him. Passive perimeter in layers as Kaitlin said. Three, take a look at this picture."

She rotated a screen showing the Supreme Autocrat at some function. Man lifted weights in a track and field manner. Muscles, but not that sharp cut to things you got from the show ponies, where they were all pretty and had almost no range of motion. Sloped shoulders and heavy upper and lower body, built almost like a wasp that way.

Power.

"Okay?" he asked, not seeing something, but absorbing everything. The woman in question was not in the picture.

"Arodd Torray is a gym rat," Messier stated. "The tops of *Traisan* culture have adapted to that, and lots of them had that physique. As do you, far more than just about anybody else on the ship. And you've leaned down from before, when you and he might have gone to the same tailor."

Oh. Right. Secondary health and breeding signals, unconsciously affecting a woman by telling her subconscious that he would father healthy children upon her. Good genes.

One little extra subtle something that could turn their head in certain circumstances.

"Think she'll fall for it?" he asked, treating these two women like his Control Officers, from another life.

"Every little bit helps, if I need you to throw yourself on that sword, sailor," Messier grinned at him. "I might suggest you look and act a little less dangerously smart than you really are, on top of it. Like the usual Gunner on a warship. The officer you replaced was aggressive, to the point her quiet nickname with the crew was *Murderhobo*. I think Nafizul the Jock might fit her expectations. Presuming ulterior motives, that is. You'll tell me. Questions?"

He paused and absorbed all that.

"One, sir," he said, waiting for her to nod. "Folks on Horwin understand just how dangerous you people really are?"

Their smiles matched his. Feral. Hungry. Mean.

"You've not had a chance to really understand Nyssa Taggart, Haque," Messier replied. "She'll scare you when she gets going on a topic."

Which was kinda scary, all by itself, considering.

18

Padraig had ridden from the surface in a palace shuttle, landing on Rafferty's dock and getting an airlock extended and deployed rather than pressurizing the entire chamber.

Just him and Irelyn, as she had insisted in private. Equerry Cayne in public, but that was *Traisa* and he got those parts.

They debarked and he led her down the long walkway, emerging into the mud room to where Kaitlin, Chance, Nafizul Haque, Zadinul Haque, and Walt Rafferty were waiting. The company told him *exactly* what they thought of Irelyn's arrival, which brought him joy.

Nice to be anticipated.

Padraig stepped to one side and introduced her to the officers, Walt and Zadi being enlisted nobodies that kind of faded out of sight quickly. As they no doubt intended.

"Captain, if I could intrude, we have a bit of a situation aft that I feel should be brought to your attention," Chance said as they paused.

Padraig turned to Nafizul, seeing how the man stacked up against the other jocks on the ground at the event he'd just come from. Greco-Roman wrestling, while it might be fun to watch, would be intense. Almost as loud and impressive as a good Sumo competition.

Still, they were all up to something.

"Mr. Haque, you take charge of seeing the Equerry's needs taken care of," he ordered in an ambiguous tone that really wasn't that ambiguous.

"Immediately, sir," Nafizul replied.

Padraig took a half-step to one side and watched the man turn on the charm. And he did it well.

"Madam Equerry, I'll be your point of contact with the crew while you are aboard," he said. "Stevedore Lynch here will supervise the Courier Pod, where we've gone ahead and put you in the main cabin for tonight so you can inspect and confirm things for your principal. If you'd care to accompany me?"

Padraig was already headed aft with Chance.

19

Padraig followed Chance to the Secondary Bridge with Bex Magorian sitting a Radio watch.

"All well?" he asked Chance as they settled in the other day office.

"Nyssa went ahead and escalated things a couple of steps based on your message, then asked Kaitlin to stage-manage," Chance grinned. "Since we know what he's previously done, I've ordered Nafizul to *make himself available,* as it were. Zadi is in the process of inventing new toys to keep watch on her. You two walked through a portable medical scanner he had on the inner airlock hatch, just as an example."

"Excellent, Chance," he replied. "I haven't been able to get any solid read on Cayne, either over dinner or on the flight up. Quiet, private woman, not given to gossiping."

"So we have no clue who she fronts for?" Chance asked.

"None," Padraig said. "But we can stay perfectly formal and polite, while setting Nafizul up to get fast and loose if he needs to. Not worried there. I assume Zadi is going to scan everything in those quarters later?"

"And strip everything for cleaning," Chance nodded. "Plus have security review all the tapes of her movement while she is aboard, making sure she doesn't wander off or leave any surprises for us. Zadi's pretty sure he baselined her and would have said something to his cousin had she been any sort of threat. Bombs, poisons, et cetera."

Padraig appreciated the paranoia on the part of his people.

"Keep it quiet and polite," he reminded her. "I can Good Cop. Nafizul can handle things as he sees fit. You supervise security and keep them on track. What do you need from me?"

Chance laughed.

"Mostly, I was protecting you from her, Padraig." Her grin was irrepressible. "Haque's a big boy. And he more closely fits *Traisan* standards of virility, at least as they see it."

"Waving a different cape under her nose?" he grinned back.

"Unless you felt the need to...*intervene*."

He laughed. Couldn't help it. He knew another captain in the fleet with a reputation as a man that would fuck any woman who slowed down enough. Didn't even need to stop running, just slow down. Amazing tactical commander and diplomat, which was why folks put up with his other *peccadilloes*.

He shook his head and took a deep breath, back to deadly serious by the intake.

"She's here," he said simply. "It may be that they are already set to run, and we might be taking on a surprise at any moment. Or setting things up for a big formal departure process with Torray announcing some sort of Olympic Games to determine the next Supreme Autocrat."

"Nyssa's passive for now, but locked on hard," Chance told him. "With you here, someone can fight the ship at any moment, even if Haque is otherwise engaged. Got everyone else poised, but no orders as yet."

"And I don't have anything to change," he agreed. "Not yet. We'll see how it shakes out with her and the folks on the ground, but keep everything sharp to move if we have to."

"They could run us down if they needed," Chance reminded him.

"Understood," Padraig replied. "Hoping it doesn't come to that."

20

Nafizul appreciated the woman's physique. Good nutrition, good genes, really sharp exercise program to maintain that shape.

At the same time, crystal hard shell. Emotionally. Intellectually. Like three centimeters of bulletproof glass.

Fortunately, it wasn't his job to seduce the woman. Made it a lot easier for him to be dangled out there like a honey pot, mostly to see how she reacted.

Usually, you used those sorts of things against amateurs. Snare someone with blackmail you could use later. Hardly ever worked with spies, partly because he'd eliminated the blackmailers twice using excessive force.

Amateurs sometimes forgot that part.

Lynch crossed them forward to the Courier Pod, then in and up. Ambassador had skylight views when they retracted steel panels overhead. And a kind of picture window with a great view of the bow.

As Ship's Gunnery Officer, he watched with a professional eye as Cayne did a quick inspection of all four decks. Storage.

Crew cabins for the support staff. Staff cabins for the Ambassador with kitchen and wardroom. Entertainment space and Ambassadorial Quarters that honestly rated 5-star against most of the best hotels he'd ever stayed in.

And supposedly the Starliner Double Pod was a whole other step above this most of the time, from what Lynch had explained.

Seducing you with glitter, he supposed. Cayne didn't seem willing to defrost the ice walls around her, but again, he was here on offer. Didn't have a mission to penetrate her operation.

However one might need to go about such a thing.

The three of them were alone, watching the picture window on Deck Four. Lynch had faded off to one side a bit. Still present, but not centered. Not like he was.

Nafizul watched Cayne turn slowly in place and take it all in. Security would, no doubt, be recording and watching everything, just in case.

He stepped up.

"Equerry Cayne, was there anything we could get you this evening?" Nafizul asked ambiguously.

Below, the pod staff had likely settled, but not gone to bed, someone always on duty against munchies in the middle of the night, and every one of them understanding a new Marshal had just come aboard and they needed to look good.

Cayne finally seemed to see him as something other than a piece of moving furniture, but he wasn't offended. Doing a job here.

"Do *A'Zedi* ambassadors always travel with immediate staffs of twenty or more?" she asked, referring to all the space on Three.

"Unlikely," Nafizul told her. "In such cases, there is a double-pod version called a Starliner with capacity for fifty.

Twenty presumes the Ambassador or senior Flag Officer hosting people for an event. A convention. A training scenario. Something where a large number of folks need to travel in better luxury than they might have in the main hull, though those cabins are normal for naval officers."

He left it at that, watching her for cues and clues.

Crystal surface. Polished smooth

A whole lot of folks could retire into exile with the Supreme Autocrat, and not be crammed in. Or a mob could be crammed in for a week, hotbunking if necessary.

What were your needs, mistress?

If there was a way to bottle that up and waft it across the space at her like a perfume, that was what he concentrated on, smiling a touch vacuously as befit a slightly-dense jock on a Transport Command vessel.

Hell, she might even fall for it.

Long pause.

"Will there be anything else, or should we retire and let you rest?" he asked. "The ship is keeping hours with the capital city below, so we'll be up early for breakfast in the main hull. As the only guest aboard, you can let the cooking crew here know your needs and they will see it done."

"I will join you for breakfast," she stated.

Nafizul took that as a dismissal and turned to Lynch. Getting a nod, he turned back to the outsider.

"Until then."

And he fled.

<h1 style="text-align:center">21</h1>

Tom understood that he was under a microscope, every second he was on the ground. Nature of the business. Fortunately, *Marrakesh* had a solid crew and he didn't worry about Boru transporting one of Torray's people to the ship.

Exactly the sort of thing you did when setting up for a formal visit.

It was late. Tom had retired with the Supreme Autocrat to a library in the palace for brandy and talk, like a couple of men in some adventure novel planning their next voyage. The room was dark with old wood stained deep and the lights turned to that comfortable level you might have in a campaign tent with one lantern on a table.

Expensive furniture, but done with a layer of rustic charm that added to the anachronistic feel. Guards by the two doors were the only interruption in the tone.

The brandy was excellent.

Tom sat on a couch across from Torray in a chair, watching him and the two guards he could see. Small talk wandered a bit.

"How do your people feel about the new treaty language I have proposed?" Torray finally asked.

If you didn't know any better, it sounded like a normal thing.

"They found it most intriguing, sir," Tom replied. "I was sent with latitude to nail down specifics and see what was needed to get it signed."

Ambiguity, because he didn't know who the guards might be loyal to. Nor who might be listening in on microphones.

"Even as big a change in the status quo as it might represent?" he pressed.

To a casual follower, it might suggest that Torray wanted a new alliance between *A'Zedi* and *Traisa*. Instead of *A'Zedi* and himself as a refuge and exile.

"It potentially opens door for *A'Zedi* to be seen in a more positive light on Zulou, sir," Tom offered. "Of course, that depends on how your people react if we can come to a formal agreement."

As in, the next Supreme Autocrat might be so pissed that we helped you escape with your life that they immediately throw in with *Wronlori* instead.

But Tom had been informed that Command, and more importantly the government, were prepared to unleash a quiet public relations campaign stressing that Torray was still around. Maybe hints of offering him a fleet later to retake things, because a hostile *Traisa* might strike at Bharani Prime as part of an attack.

And there would already be major fleet elements protecting that world anyway.

"Captain Boru," Torray hared off on a tangent. "He impressed me earlier. What is his ship like?"

"Last of the M-boats, sir," Tom replied. "A Tactical Transport hauling two pods to deliver me to your court with a certain level of style. Not a particularly fast vessel, but a well-founded one with a top-notch crew that have impressed me during the time I've been with them."

"Old and slow?" Torray pressed.

Tom shrugged.

"We build much better vessels today, Supreme Autocrat," he offered, mostly to remind whoever was listening that the P-boat cruisers were coming on line these days. "*Marrakesh* is older than I am, by hull, but well maintained."

You are not outrunning a Super-Cruiser, buddy. Nor outfighting one. Probably, anyway.

Tom had caught hints from both Boru and his new Gunnery Officer Haque that they weren't all that impressed by *Crimson Firebird*. At the same time, most of this crew had once taken on a *Wronlori* Leviathan and won, so Tom wouldn't discount them in a battle.

"I shall take a tour of the vessel," Torray announced.

Foregone conclusion, with Cayne doing groundwork already, but Tom supposed that the man was playing to the galleries as much as he had been.

All the galaxy is a stage, and we are merely players.

"And I am at your disposal to round out the final details of the treaty language, sir," he reminded.

"Business can wait," Torray waved a negligent hand. "I find myself wishing to measure *A'Zedi* on the value of one, old M-boat, in order to see how good they might be."

Tom nodded and let that one go.

He wasn't sure that *Marrakesh* could just sail away with Torray aboard and not risk interception, but it let the man set the ground now to do things later. Without others watching over his shoulder.

That might be important.

22

Padraig caught Taggart's simple note that Nafizul had slept in his own quarters. Alone. It made him smile.

How do you outthink a spy? Especially someone who might not be?

Plan ahead, and have people prepared to react.

He'd set an early alarm today and been close to first in line for fresh biscuits, even after an hour of reviewing paperwork, but Padraig knew that today would either be insane, or dull, with no chance of anything in the middle.

He had a spy aboard, after all.

She joined him for breakfast, but Kaitlin was stage-managing. Chance had the bridge at the moment, so Padraig had invited Nyssa. Himself and three women.

Far too early to be a gossipy brunch, but doing it in the wardroom with the crew around at once should put her at ease, and put her on display.

"Do you always eat with the common sailors?" Cayne asked as they got settled, having gone through the line and carried her own tray, something that she might not have done in a while from her response.

"There are times when a formal meal with my officers is important," Padraig replied. "At least weekly, with everyone putting on their nice uniforms. Some evenings I have working dinners with one of more of my officers or senior enlisted experts to talk business. And some meals I take here."

He watched the sourness never quite make it to her eyes, but linger close.

"Padraig is not some terrible patriarch who must maintain an emotional distance from his crew, Irelyn," Kaitlin offered in her role as translator. Culture more than language, but language as well. "This is a relatively small ship for overall crew, being a transport instead of a warship."

"And even on a Line Cruiser, I wouldn't change much," he interjected. "While my open door policy is generally for more senior people, there have been two occasions where one of the most junior sailors had something that they felt would have to be raised to my level anyway, and chose to approach me quietly. A well run ship runs itself. That starts at the top. My people know how things should operate, so they can make those decisions. As long as they understand potential repercussions."

One sailor that had fallen in love with a local and wanted to quit the navy and stay with her. Eventually, he'd come around and returned to his senses. The other had gotten news of a tragedy in the family and asked permission for extended leave to deal with it, which had eventually involved departing the navy, but done with all the correct paperwork ahead of time to make separation easier.

"Supreme Autocrat Torray wishes to tour this vessel," Irelyn stated bluntly.

"Formal visit by visiting head of state," Padraig replied evenly. "Full honors. Dress uniforms pressed and cleaned. You'll want to sample the cooking staff in the pod, as I suspect they're better than my main wardroom, but again who fixes his dinner is flexible. He may have a personal chef that comes aboard and supervises. Or cooks. How can we best show the *A'Zedi* flag to impress and honor the Supreme Autocrat?"

She ate some, thinking. Possibly expecting a much more formal argument in a conference room, taking days to get this far because everybody had checklists to work through.

He wondered if she wasn't part of what was coming, after all, and had been sent to distract.

Or didn't really like the *Directorate* and didn't trust them to be helpful. Padraig got that, too. The Supreme Autocrat was probably the only one he'd get a straight answer out of, if not Cayne while she was here.

And he wasn't about to suggest anything first.

"Full day visit, or overnight?" Irelyn asked, back to some mental checklist it seemed.

"My orders were to transport Division Marshal Ussher and place my crew and vessel at his disposal," Padraig reminded her. "How do we make him look good? How do we make you look good?"

She had obviously been expecting more ego here. He saw surprise again, for almost long enough to actually categorize it, then the hard eyes were back. She paused to take in Nyssa, then turned to Kaitlin beside her.

"Just like that?" she asked.

"Yes," Kaitlin replied. "Just like that."

Hard eyes turned back to Padraig.

"I will convey your offer to the Supreme Autocrat," she

said, possibly ceding the field of battle here, but he was winning on the technicality of giving her most of what she wanted.

Within reason.

The proof would be in the pudding at some point.

23

———————

Division Marshal Thomas Ussher had on the fancy uniform today. Arodd Torray didn't believe in fucking around, and had taken the report from he Equerry and scheduled a tour of *Marrakesh* on their fourth day in harbor.

Boru had basically gotten enough warning to clean things, but Tom was pretty sure he'd been doing that with some level of monomaniacal frenzy anyway. There had been a quick update from the man about Cayne's visit, filtered of course because others might be listening.

A ship on the spot, but prepared for it. No shenanigans on that trip, but Tom had to shake his head—only on the inside considering the company—and smile ruefully. All the shenanigans were accompanying him on this shuttle, currently lifting to orbit.

Or maybe yacht was a better term for it. Utter elegance and luxury, though from what he'd seen of the man in three days, Torray might take this thing out annually at most. Possibly on a hunting trip before it dropped him and a few friends in the middle of nowhere for them to hike back out later.

83

Gold and platinum everything, matched well against bronze and dark wood. Forest greens. Storm blue-grays. That indigo you got right at that moment when the sun vanished.

Totally out of character for Arodd Torray, save that he was in his finery today. Dark Green, trimmed in blue and red. Calf boots with pants tucked in. Thigh length jacket with equipment belt, single breasted over a black shirt. No hats, but Tom was given to understand that they wore them for outdoor events.

Not peacocks, because not nearly bright enough or loud enough, but the personalities around him made up for it. The Supreme Autocrat had brought with him a significant chunk of the formal Household.

High Steward Greer Rownett, something like a Chief of Staff.

High Chamberlain Taran Severt, the Protocol Officer in charge of diplomacy, among other things.

Private Secretary Kennet Sanders.

Comptroller of the Household Ristoph Baker. The Accountant.

Equerry Irelyn Cayne, who was technically in charge of transport, but appeared to be Torray's troubleshooter.

The only Important Personage™ left out appeared to be the Mistress at Arms, Ana Pera, whose writ ran from supervising the bodyguard to running the Interior Ministry in charge of the various secret police.

Tom was just as happy not to have that woman around. Reminded him too much of a gila monster sunning itself on a rock.

More interestingly, none of the folks taking the tour had aides or their own bodyguards. The only spare people around were crew on the yacht, flying it or handling personal needs, and all looked at little queasy at the situation.

Six bigshots on a shuttle. No escorts of any kind, save the warships in orbit that Tom was certain all had extra guns unlimbered and ready to fire on *Marrakesh*. Or any other threat.

And, more interestingly, Torray had made it a point of honor that nobody brought personal weapons with them on this trip, as it would supposedly be an insult to their hosts to show up armed.

Tom wasn't about to say one thing on the topic, one way or the other. Diplomacy meant knowing when the shut the hell up, too.

Fortunately, they'd kind of lost track of him, fussing at one another like wet hens as the yacht lifted out of the atmosphere.

Just as well. This was going to be interesting.

24

Nyssa had taken one look at the message from Marshal Ussher and politely sounded the general alert. Captain Boru and Commander Messier had been supervising things for the visit. He paused on the screen she was watching and approached the comm.

"Radio?" he asked simply.

Nyssa read him the roster of guests from the vessel currently lifting off.

"That's it?" he asked.

"No bodyguards, sir," Nyssa pointed out. "Shuttle crew of six, all of whom are assigned to that vessel permanently. No aides. No goons. Nobody but those six."

"Make sure Nafizul is on duty and on alert," Captain Boru replied.

"He just slid into his station next to me, sir," Nyssa said. "I assume we're keeping this quiet?"

"Completely," he told her. "Do not open missile launcher hatches or power up turrets, but everything to stay exactly one step short of that until we have a better handle on the situation."

"Got it covered, sir. Wanted you to know."

"Keep up the good work, Nyssa. Out."

She turned to the Gunner and smiled.

"Threats to the shuttle?" he asked immediately, scanning his boards.

"None detected, but this is out of the ordinary, Gunner," she told him. "Originally, we'd been expecting twenty or so visitors. They sent the Big Six and nobody else."

"I'm not seeing the Mistress at Arms, Radio."

"That's what caused me to raise the alert level, sir," she said. "Do we need to provide them some?"

"Stand by," he said. She watched him dial.

"Security. Farrell."

"Round up all of your people and get them armed," he ordered the woman in charge of that sort of thing. "Stun weapons only, and tell them that they might be doing bodyguard work, rather than our guests being a threat. I'm sending Zadi down with orders to count the visitors' teeth and tell me what they had for breakfast."

"On it, sir."

Nyssa nodded.

Nafizul studied her for a long moment.

"Would you have any way of being able to determine if we were about to be attacked in harbor?" he asked delicately.

She considered it. Hadn't broken their codes yet, but they hadn't been here long enough to get a solid sample to work from, either.

How could she manage?

"Traffic volume analysis might do it," she offered, watching his eyes cross in confusion. "There is a baseline amount of constant noise in harbor. If someone were about to launch an attack, I would expect a sudden jump in encrypted communications among stations and ships. I can watch for that."

"Do that," he ordered. "Our job right now is making sure nobody sneaks up on the ship while the Captain and XO are hosting visitors. Zarah, how much can you prepare without actually giving anything away?"

Nyssa liked that he'd relaxed enough to lock in as part of the team. *Murderhobo* had never gotten there, but she'd simply been the wrong personality for *Marrakesh*.

"Engineering, Ahearn."

"It's Squire Halloran," Zarah told the Engineer. "I need all generators warm but not ramped up. Similarly, all engines and other systems prepared. We don't want to suddenly get bright on any scanners someone is pointed at us, but I want to be able to slam the rotary thrusters into gear on a moment's notice. Maybe go to Ghostdrives without warning."

"We expecting anything, Helm?" Ahearn asked carefully.

"Negative, Knight," Nyssa spoke loud enough for the microphone to pick up. "This is Radio and Gunner running an exercise that will verge right over onto active measures."

And Jareth Ahearn was a smart man. Plus, he knew the schedule of events today.

"Stand by, Helm," he replied. "I'll cycle them all on over the next ten minutes then hold them at baseline."

"Exactly what I needed, Engineer," Zarah noted, all grim-faced and game-faced.

Nyssa sucked down a hard breath and studied her boards, then started making adjustments in who she was listening to.

And who she was watching.

25

Cameron Farrell was *Marrakesh*'s only permanent security trooper. Everybody else had secondary jobs, like Trinh Hoàng who worked primarily for the Quartermaster. And didn't have her Light Disruptor Cannon strapped across her back today.

Didn't stop her bitching, though.

Trinh and her were the only two in public, with everyone else currently staged in a couple of places nearby, watching monitors and following everything. Ready, but not up in anybody's faces about things.

She'd seen the weightlifter bods. All of them folks were gym rats of one sort or another. But they were also politicians, so didn't spend entire days on the gun range like she did. Or the dojo floor polishing a variety of open-hand and weapon forms.

Trinh would just take out an ankle or a knee to get you down to her level if she had to start shit. Then get mean. She was like that.

Cousin Haque meandered close with a scanner in one hand.

Unfortunate nickname he'd earned for being 'The Other Haque' when the new Gunner came aboard. And ranked him.

Plus, stories of navigational failures had gotten around.

"Just you two?" Zadi asked, glancing at things.

"Within reach," Cam corrected him.

Zadi paused, then achieved enlightenment and nodded.

"Gotcha. Baselined the one woman," he continued. "Will get the others on the way in and out."

Cam glanced over at the Captain watching. Messier had returned to the bridge with most of the command team. Captain and Stevedore were in charge here.

Cam didn't say anything. Captain didn't, either. But he'd briefed her. Not everyone might be on that shuttle when it departed.

At least that was the rumor. Her job was Security. Capital Letters there. With Trinh to gnaw on ankles.

It was sliding into the bay now. Tight fit, but Air Boss had said they could make it work once he moved *Roadrunner* and *Flight of Fancy* around some. Big, clear wall let her watch.

Pilot knew her stuff. Delicate into the gap and down, magnets locking it in place. And the airlock tunnel swung out instead of pressurizing the bay. Just like last time. Set Cousin Haque up to scan people in sequence.

Cam moved to a corner out of the way. Trinh took the other one. Guard duty against yahoos yahooing, but that was her job about here.

26

Padraig greeted Marshal Ussher first out of the hatch, both of them in their fanciest duds and the man coming to rest next to him to form a receiving line for visiting politicians. He wasn't surprised that Torray came through next, trailed immediately by Irelyn.

What he did find interesting was that she was the only female of the six visitors. As hard as the men, though not as musclebound. In this company, that just meant that she wasn't taking any hormone supplements to build muscle mass. Woman still had that body, just feminine.

Mostly.

Unarmed meant that he had tucked Farrell into a corner with her sidekick. Zadinul Haque was over out of the way with Walt Rafferty, like maybe he was 2IC of the flight deck, instead of sensors spy.

Nyssa would be reading those scanner results in real time, with her comm to warn folks if she needed.

And no chef, but Padraig wasn't sure who would be cooking dinner for the man and his staff. Fortunately, it was just after lunch and they had a few hours before dinner became a question.

"Supreme Autocrat, it is a pleasure to see you again. Welcome aboard *Marrakesh*," Padraig said to the man, unsurprised when Torray walked right up and shook his hand.

Firm, but not that bonecrushing ego thing that some men did.

Small men, uncertain of themselves and attempting to intimidate people around them because they couldn't impress them.

"I wished to see what one old, M-class boat—Tom Ussher's words—was like, Boru," Torray announced with a knowing grin.

Padraig shook hands with the others, including Cayne, both pretending this was her first visit.

Greer Rownett was the Chief of Staff as High Steward. The man who controlled access to the Supreme Autocrat and ran the household like a small corporation from the notes Padraig had absorbed.

Taran Severt , the High Chamberlain, did diplomacy, and might have been a bit put out that Torray was secretly negotiating a treaty with *A'Zedi*, leaving him in the dark.

Private Secretary Kennet Sanders might have been a Consigliere, but didn't look like a leg-breaker when the boss needed someone assassinated. Merely the guy who could argue with him behind closed doors.

The Comptroller looked like an accountant. And not one of the dangerous ones. Merely the guy who killed people with numbers and spreadsheets.

The Equerry stood out for her biological gender and that bright edge of deadliness, but she had subsumed most of her femininity around these hard-ass men, and that was much more obvious when she was in her proper context.

All of them got introduced to Kaitlin and made the mistake, not counting Cayne and Torray, of seeing her as some sort of middle-aged *Housefrau*. Padraig didn't correct them.

And he and Marshal Ussher had swapped roles here, which was just odd, but Torray was driving it.

"What can I show you first, sir?" Padraig asked.

Very few military secrets here, and almost all of them wrapped up in heads anyway, so they could see the last of the M-boats and not learn much.

"Ready missile storage and a launcher, Captain," the Supreme Autocrat announced.

Not where Padraig would have expected, but why the hell not?

"This way, folks," he said, stopping himself short of saying *gentlemen* as he had one biologically female person present.

Port Main Battery was closer, so he went that way, hoping that Radio was listening and warning people. Or that they were sharp.

The missiles were beasts. Five meters long, with the front half of that being the warhead. Solid fuel core aft, burning out from a central gap once lit and accelerating until triggered or it reached burnout and separated.

"This is a Six, Captain?" Torray asked, touching one on a rack.

"Affirmative, sir," Padraig replied. "The nosecone will separate into six equal parts and spread like a shotgun blast. Given that those are solid alloy, traveling at a tiny fraction of light-speed when they impact, kinetic energy gets translated into damage and plasma. We keep a few Threes in case we ever encounter something large enough to warrant, same as we have

Nines for engaging smaller targets. Escorts might also carry Twelves for defending against swarms."

"Are your crews any good, Boru?" the man asked bluntly.

"We can hold our own on tonnage," Padraig fired back.

That battle against the Leviathan had been luck and planning, rather than a slugging match. But he was also willing to bend luck into his favor, like the *Northwind* mission where Maddox had had a stroke of genius to lay a minefield ahead of time.

Choosing the death ground, according to the ancient tomes.

From there, forward to the Twin Heavy Particle Cannon turret, itself clean and no crew grab-assing anywhere it sight. Which was not always a given with those people.

A peek into a couple of workshops and spaces and they ended up forward.

"Marshal on the bridge," Nyssa called out as they entered.

As expected, nods but everyone was on duty, so Chance was the only one who addressed them.

"My First Officer," Padraig said. "Commander Chance Messier."

"And the others?" Torray asked, looking around.

"Gunnery Officer Haque. Radio Officer Taggart. Helm Halloran. Coxswain Whelan supervising Engineering."

Torray took it all in. Padraig noted that everyone had shifted screens around from what he usually saw when looking over shoulders, so they were hiding how hyped up all of them were for trouble. Which he appreciated.

Torray didn't have a baseline to compare, so he absorbed it and nodded.

"Truly an impressive vessel, Captain Boru," he announced to the room in a voice intended to be heard by everyone. "I believe Stevedore Lynch supervises the Courier Pod that is our next stop?"

"Indeed she does, Supreme Autocrat," Padraig replied. "Kaitlin?"

"This way," Kaitlin said, leading the mob back out.

Padraig got a critical glance, deadly serious at odds with the rest of the tour, as Torray ended up following his own staff out of the bridge.

But his people were ready.

Whatever was coming.

27

———————

Tom had had a couple of moments of a really good pucker, but Boru's people had stepped it up. All of them. And he'd been around them for a month at this point, so it was extra gratifying that they'd been sandbagging *him* and had a whole other gear on top of what he'd already seen on the flight out.

Lynch led them aft. Tom noted the two women providing overall security, one almost as tall as him and the other who looked like she'd had to get up on her toes to meet minimum height requirements to enlist. Both had that extra gear going today, too.

Courier pod hadn't changed. Someone must have said something, because the staff had been baking biscuits and cookies, possibly timing both to pull them fresh from the stove as everyone entered below, because there was a side table set up with water, juice, and steaming pastries.

Steaming.

He slipped over and grabbed a cookie first because the others were all bound by a protocol that didn't include him.

Fresh chocolate chip cookies, still melty. One of life's great pleasures and the cooks had figured that out about him on the flight.

Munch.

The others caught on and followed the Supreme Autocrat over. Tom got a grin nobody else could see while the rest were busy. And Torray only took one cookie, eating it quickly while the others lingered at their choices.

Boru and the small Security trooper were off to one side. The tall one was opposite, eyes like a hungry cat watching the room. Tom finished his cookie and watched a change come over the Supreme Autocrat.

The man smiled. It was not a pleasant smile, but it was a thing filled with some sort of unholy glee.

"You, what is your name?" Torray pointed to the corner.

"Lead Expert Farrell, sir," the tall woman replied, eyes never pausing as they tracked the entire room. "Security Lead, *Marrakesh*."

The one trooper always on duty.

"Excellent, Farrell," Torray announced. "You will stand here."

He pointed to a spot midway between Tom and the Supreme Autocrat. About where a formal bodyguard would stand in uncertain or public circumstances.

Boru saw it immediately, too. As did the tiny woman with the dangerous eyes next to him.

Interestingly, Torray's people were distracted by cookies and biscuits, but that had to be pure luck and timing on Lynch and Boru's part.

Didn't it?

Tom found that suddenly he wasn't so certain.

Torray clapped his hands once for attention, but that was

for his people. Tom's people—and he was in charge around here—were already three steps ahead.

Locked in hard. Ready for combat, and he'd seen the two women move enough to understand that they could take any of the strangers by themselves.

Farrell's stance suggested that all the rest of her people might be standing just outside the hatch, ready to pour in if they had to.

That extra gear he'd only discovered in the last two hours.

He found his own smile, but it wasn't as predatory as the Supreme Autocrat's.

Yet.

The *Tyrannical Household of Traisa* all turned around and woke up to trouble, almost in perfect synch like a chorus line. With yummies stuffed in mouths as people chewed furiously.

"I have an announcement to make," Arodd Torray seemed to take great pleasure in his words.

But then, it almost felt like the detective's big reveal at the end of a whodunit. Slightly larger scale here.

Everyone fell to stillness, with *A'Zedi* primed and *Traisa* confused. Probably for the best.

"I would like to share with you one of the most valuable insights my immediate predecessor as Supreme Autocrat shared with me, there at the end," Torray continued, sober at least, but not deadly.

Farrell had that covered.

"He told me that being Supreme Autocrat of the *Enlightened Tyranny of Traisa* was like living with a nymphomaniac," Torray spoke. "Utterly fantastic. For the first two weeks. He was not wrong."

Pause. Swallow. Catch up if you can, but none of the Household even twitched otherwise, facing the only two armed people in the room. Also not an accident, in retrospect. But then, the man had reached out quietly and negotiated terms for retirement in exile, rather than dying in office like all of his predecessors had.

Some had even died of old age.

"You will note the circumstances," Torray bore in on them, Tom and his people seemingly forgotten.

No, Tom and Boru forgotten. The visitors suddenly tracked the two women a lot closer.

"Sir, what's going on?" the High Chamberlain asked carefully.

Taran Severt. A shade taller than Torray, but the same general shape. Maybe not as weightlifter build, but muscles and hard. Like all of them.

Farrell and her partner didn't seem concerned. Even outnumbered in here.

"I have decided that I have been Supreme Autocrat for long enough," Torray announced. "It is my intension to resign my position and go into permanent exile from the *Tyranny*. *A'Zedi* has agreed to provide me refuge."

Tom was watching with poker-player eyes, looking for tells. Every player had them. The very best players could even fake them, so he didn't put much credence into anything these five were telling him. Not yet.

Cayne had either missed what was coming, or could react that much faster. She relaxed a shade.

The others were a little gut-punched. Back foot and needing a moment to recover.

"Now?" Cayne asked.

"Now," Torray agreed, eyeing the woman closer. "I will not be returning, so if you chose to accompany me, you would also be facing a permanent exile. I have planned well ahead. The

Treasury has not been looted, but the Autocrat himself has access to certain funds that have been invested in ways that I control them and none of you can reach. I will not want."

"What about the office?" the High Steward asked.

Green Rownett. A pretty good political warrior, but Tom had found him a little too full of himself and his position. Looked down his nose at everyone else a little more than Tom would have found acceptable if he was a local.

Or staying for any period of time, because that much was obvious.

Hell, he'd only be out one suitcase of clothes if all else failed, because he technically hadn't been accredited yet, so he hadn't moved himself to the ground. And had packed his important things back up to the ship with him in a diplomatic pouch this morning.

Even if everyone had been caught by surprise.

"I will be forfeiting it," Torray told them. "And I had no interest in one of you killing me to take power. Personally, whichever of you takes over after this, I suggest that you look at creating a retirement option, because ten years seems to be the point at which burnout overcomes excitement. When the nymphomania simply isn't worth it. But that's not my problem. It's yours. All of you."

"You think you can just flee from *Traisa* and escape?" Rownett asked, finding a shade of a growl.

"None of you are the Supreme Autocrat," Torray sneered. "Not yet, anyway. How long will it take one of you to grab those reins and hold them, in order to do something about it?"

Tom appreciated the subtlety of bringing his all of top lieutenants aboard, without aides or guards, then tossing that cookie into the scrum like a puck.

All five were suddenly eyeballing one another sidelong.

Tom kept his chuckles to himself, because they didn't even had belt knives to sort it out on the deck here or the flight home.

And that trip ought to be a hoot. Pity he couldn't be a fly on a wall to watch that shit unravel.

It would be a feeding frenzy, and Torray had apparently stolen a march on everyone.

"Oh, one other thought," Torray said, dropping that other shoe. If that shoe was made of concrete and falling from orbit. "You'll note that Ana Pera didn't accompany us to orbit. She's back in the palace right now, technically exercising supreme authority in my name while I am here. If you gave her any hint of what was about to happen, would she even let you get back to the ground alive?"

"We're supposed to fight it out right here, while you watch?" Severt snarled. "Kill one another for the position?"

"On the contrary, I want the five of you to return to Jensen with your own conspiracy of silence," Torray scourged them with his words and smile. "Land on my personal pad, then lock everything down so you can slip into the palace itself without Ana being any the wiser. My advice would be for you to team up to take her out first, but that's just a suggestion. You might even prefer her being the Supreme Autocrat."

Tom watched that moment of horror wash over the group.

He'd met Pera. Rabid Piranha of a woman, just measuring her personality. Not unattractive in person, if you felt like fucking a box of rusty knives.

None of the others apparently felt that way, either.

Severt finally registered that Torray wasn't alone in this, turning to study Tom.

"Your conspiracy?" he asked.

"Arodd Torray contacted us and asked for asylum," Tom replied evenly. "We proposed exile instead, on an *Unaffiliated* world which would temporarily draw *Directorate* protection, allowing him to make subsequent arrangements to vanish entirely. The hope was that all the usual palace coups and civil wars here might be somewhat mitigated, as *A'Zedi* maintains a studied neutrality in trade and military affairs with regards to the *Enlightened Tyranny of Traisa*. Until this moment, I had been uncertain how the situation would unfold, to be honest, so I'm almost as surprised as you to be standing here."

Not that it would save him from personal enemies, but Tom didn't have much longer before he retired anyway, so he could vanish into the weeds if he could pull this off, cloaked in glory and then shadows.

The five didn't seem impressed.

Torray, master showman that he was, turned to Kaitlin Lynch.

"Madame Stevedore, might I impose on your hospitality to see this group fed and catered to for a time, while I retire to the vessel itself?" he asked, all courtly charm. "The ground would have concerns if the shuttle were to return so quickly, triggering alarms that they wouldn't be able to negate nor control."

Tom watched the woman turn to Boru and get a quick nod. As she should, because this was right out at the edge of what Tom figured he could finesse with the folks back on Horwin.

And then, only if they could pull it off.

"I will see what we can arrange, sir," Lynch replied, turning to the others now and ignoring the soon-to-be-former Supreme Autocrat of *Traisa*.

"I'm certain that the staff are prepared to respond quickly, but obviously were not prepared for this particular situation," Lynch said, turning on her own charm. "If I could continue to distract you with baked goods and juice for a time, I will let them know."

"Stevedore," a female voice announced. "I've updated them. Expected delivery of early dinner is forty minutes."

Sounded like the Radio Officer. Tom was glad she was listening.

A hatch opened and eight more sailors entered, including one of the biggest humans Tom had ever met. Fairy tales would call him an ogre.

"Farrell," the intercom continued, "I've routed your team in."

"Excellent work, my new friends," Torray announced. "To my old comrades, I truly do wish you the best."

"Arodd," Equerry Cayne suddenly spoke up. "Permanent exile and vanish from history?"

"That is the plan, Irelyn," he replied. "Rather sorry that I couldn't warn you, but you understand the reasons and implications, I'm certain."

"Are guests welcome?" she asked, throwing the emotional gravity in the room further off.

"*Forever*, Irelyn," he reminded her. "Not only not come back. Not look back. New life. New identity papers. **Gone**."

"There is about to be a bloodbath in your old palace, Arodd," she reminded him. "This might be the perfect chance to get out alive."

Torray turned to Tom.

"Two to travel?" he asked.

"We're prepared, sir," Tom said.

"If you could take charge here?" he asked, then turned to Boru. "Captain, I find myself at your disposal."

28

Padraig was not a poker player, but he could recognize a masterclass when one unfolded in front of him.

Hoàng accompanied them into the main hull, where two more troopers were guarding the hatch already.

"Just how prepared were you, Boru?" Torray asked as the four of them headed forward at a brisk pace.

Him. Trinh. Torray. Cayne.

"I have a sharp crew, sir," Padraig replied evasively. "And Ussher has kept us on our toes during the flight out."

"I see. You saw what was coming?"

"We had a rough idea of the what, Mister Torray," Padraig said, trying to find a term for ex-Supreme Autocrat. "Not the how or the when. You arriving without guards or aides caused my people to step up their planning. Mostly, we've tried to be ready to protect you and the ship. Not sure how it will go down when we suddenly break orbit and start running."

"I would like to record a message to be broadcast," Torray said. "Declaring Tom *persona non grata* and immediately ordering him to depart the system under threat of sanction.

Pity I can't figure out how to have the shuttle do that as they depart."

Padraig paused in the corridor. The two strangers stopped and turned to face him, accidentally turning their backs on Hoàng.

Her position wasn't an accident, facing him from behind them.

"You are never returning home once word gets out, correct?" he confirmed, away from the other four yahoos about to get messy with one another.

"No Supreme Autocrat has ever made it out alive, Boru," Torray replied. "I'm simply getting as much of a headstart as I can manage."

He turned to Cayne next. Impressive woman, but Padraig had no idea what was driving her, save that perhaps these two had some sort of relationship that went beyond business.

None of his business, as long as it didn't threaten his ship.

"You will also be under sanction?" Padraig asked her.

"Palace bloodbath," she repeated from before. "Probably by dawn. The only real question is who wins. I'm not even sure if those four or Pera manage. Might be another dark horse somewhere who takes out the shuttle and then palace when nobody is looking."

"Did you know it was coming?" he asked her point blank.

"Something was happening," she acknowledged. "Arodd had been acting peculiar. I suspected that he was about to sign a new treaty with *A'Zedi* to join the war and hit *Wronlori* with a surprise attack somewhere. Not this."

Padraig was on the spot, but made a decision.

"Mister Torray, that message can probably be sent from the shuttle," he said. "My Radio Officer is exceptional at what she does. Nyssa, can you meet me in my office? Chance, stay on the bridge and keep us poised on the verge of alert."

"Understood, Captain," Nyssa replied instantly on the intercom, so she'd been following them on internal monitors. "She's nodding."

Because Nyssa Taggart was that good.

Padraig started walking again.

Now they just had to pull it off.

29

———

Nyssa had left Bex in charge, with orders to escalate to Messier at the drop of a hat. Safer that way, because the Commander knew her shit.

Captain and guests were in his office when she got there, Trinh in a corner being invisible like she did.

"Mister Torray, Radio Officer Nyssa Taggart," Captain said. "Mistress Cayne, you've already met."

Nyssa nodded and moved to the side wall, parade rest and out of Trinh's way.

"Radio, how good is security on the shuttle?" Captain asked her.

"Adequate, but not much more, sir," she replied.

Adequate to keep most people out.

The ones who didn't have tools like hers for penetrating supposedly secured systems.

"Could you insert controls into the vessel to broadcast a message without them being able to do anything about it?" Captain asked.

"Aye, sir."

Easier to simply agree. If the strangers didn't know how hard most people would find that, better for everyone.

"Could we hold conversations, Taggart?" Arodd Torray asked. "Somehow fool everyone into thinking I was aboard that shuttle?"

Nyssa paused. Considered.

Pain in the ass, unless she had a transmitter she completely owned. Then linked it with a tight-beam laser on the ship. Easiest to do if it was on the dorsal somewhere.

She turned to Captain Boru.

"I might need to place a device on the outer hull of the shuttle, sir," she noted, leaving off all the details of how.

"You have probably two hours before we send them home, Radio," he replied. "Make it happen."

She nodded and headed for the hatch.

Hopefully, the cousins could pull it off.

30

Nafizul had joined Taggart in a small conference space and heard her explanation. Utterly insane. At the same time, he'd actually done it more than once, and had to assume that this woman had read enough of his file to know that.

He turned to his cousin.

"How big will it be?" Nafizul asked. "And include magnetic controls that can cause it to fall off later so nobody can find it."

Zadi was already nodding. He held up both hands and enclosed a volume a little wider than a bagel and rectangular.

"This do?" Zadi asked. "Maybe a kilogram or so, overall."

"You go build it," Nafizul ordered. "Right now. Time's burning."

Zadi was gone that quickly. Nafizul turned to Air Boss Rafferty.

"How do I lower it from above and attach it to that shuttle?" Nafizul asked.

Rafferty was a pilot, but he'd been promoted and cross-trained to handle mechanic and administrative tasks as well, and that took brains.

"Radio, I need a scalable bay layout in three dimensions," he told Taggart.

Nafizul watched her bring one up, then hand Rafferty the controller. The Air Boss moved things around a bit, then zoomed the view in.

"Top of the dorsal engine array work?" he asked.

Nafizul studied the image.

The yacht had three engines, arranged in a triangle around the hull externally. Two down with landing gear that folded up into the housing, and the third centerline overhead. Two stubby wings and a matching fin for control surfaces in atmosphere. Bridge space actually rear, up a deck just in front of the top engine, almost like some smaller sailing vessels he'd been aboard in his time.

That let the boss have a fantastic view out the bow, but it put the crew a little too close to where he was likely to make noise.

Taggart saw his grimace.

"Sir?"

"I need a distraction," he told her. Told them. "Noise that will hide what I'm doing."

"Connecting the boarding tunnel will make noise," Rafferty replied. "Especially if I do a half-assed job of it. How long do you need?"

"They'll see something out the window."

"Close the blast panels," Taggart replied. "That lets you move around, as long as the crew aren't watching. If you time it to when the folks are boarding, they should be distracted."

Nafizul studied the layout.

There were about a dozen better ways to do something like

this, but all of them presupposed more time to plan the approach and get more sophisticated equipment that was better camouflaged.

But then, from what he'd heard, the folks on the shuttle might not make much noise about the Supreme Autocrat not being aboard, since that one Interior Ministry woman might hit them with Surface-To-Air missiles so she could take over the entire government herself.

"Best we can do," Nafizul decided. "How do I make my approach?"

"Here's an overhead access tunnel that lets us get to the crane controls when we want to pull maintenance..." Rafferty began.

Nafizul sat and absorbed it. They'd get one chance to do it quiet.

Or do it wrong.

<h1 style="text-align:center">31</h1>

Tom appreciated having more goons than politicians handy. And folks ready for violence, from the way Farrell and the others watched but didn't move much.

Primed. That extra gear.

Lynch had gotten everyone into a conference room. The four remaining players had taken cardinal points around it, both short ends, both wide sides.

Tom ended up sitting between Severt and Comptroller Baker. Farrell was close enough behind him that he could smell her.

Exactly what he preferred, given the situation.

"What happens next?" Severt demanded in a formal tone. Not nice. Not even polite, but not raging.

The crew were the only ones armed, and even then gave off a hint that they'd go bare-handed at the politicians if provoked.

"As I noted earlier, High Chamberlain, I was as surprised as you that it was happening today," Tom offered diplomatically. "Not that Torray wanted out, but that he was already moving.

I presume one of you or someone in the palace had suddenly escalated their own maneuvers?"

Nobody took the bait. Just as well. Get them all home and let them sort each other out.

Euphemistically.

"And he's gone?" Rownett asked.

"We'll send you home, then I presume *Marrakesh* will hit the sky running as soon as you clear the bay," Tom acknowledged. "Since nobody can give the fleet orders at the moment, we can hopefully disappear and Torray becomes my problem."

"Yours?" Private Secretary Sanders pressed.

"We're putting him on an *Unaffiliated* world," Tom said. "And guarding him there. Politely, he will be a songbird in a gilded cage, and I will become his jailer. He can't leave, because the fleet will be protecting that world."

"How long?" Severt asked.

"A year," Tom told him. "Maybe two. Depends on how quickly *Traisa* settles down with a new Supreme Autocrat in charge. My promise to you folks is that he's out of your lives for good. At some point, he gets a new name and a new legend and vanishes entirely. Lives out his life on a beach somewhere. Or whatever retired Supreme Autocrats might do."

None had ever gotten out of the palace alive, so Tom didn't know what Torray might accomplish. Or where.

Didn't really care, either. *Traisa* could accept it, or they could get pissy about things.

A'Zedi Intelligence had quiet plans to set the man loose and maybe offer him resources for revenge, if *Traisa* decided to declare war on the *Directorate*. Fleets. Assassins. All sorts of trouble that could be unleashed.

"And our flight home?" Rownett demanded.

"I will let all of you in on a little secret," Tom told them, looking around. "I have no more interest in Pera taking over than any of you do. If she'd have come, I might have made a case for her to suffer an accident before you left. Any of you would be far preferable to her. I'd like you to get to the ground so you can take her out, but I can't offer any resources there. Then I'd like you to understand that we're doing this thing—the *Directorate* is—because Torray asked for a way out when there wasn't one. Whichever of you are next, maybe start that process as he suggested? I understand and appreciate that you killed your kings and extended royal family more than a century ago for a reason, but all you did was replace them with a different kind of king, if I can be so crass. The *Directorate* has a group in charge, so things have to be negotiated and folks can retire when they feel like they're done. Or need to be replaced without splattering their brains all over a wall somewhere."

Tom left off at that point and watched them watching him.

And each other. Someone had been watching, because a hatch opened and stewards were suddenly arriving with food. And had been paying attention, because everything was common troughs with spoons, so nobody was getting poisoned.

Or everyone was, including him.

He took the first spoonful of goulash onto his bowl and reached for the bread. It was going to be a tense meal, but hopefully they would all get through it without Security having to whomp anyone.

Because things were already past *Diplomatic Incident* here.

32

Nafizul had pulled open a panel enough to look through the crack and watch to the flight bay below him. This whole upper section he was in had been depressurized to match the bay. Zadi's doohickey was in a bag outside his spacesuit and a rope winch was already tacked to the bulkhead, ready to drop.

"Radio, I'm in position," he said quietly into his suit mic.

She swore that nobody on that shuttle could tap their communications. Wasn't a life and death mistake, but needed to be handled with professionalism, if they were going to pull this off and buy time to run.

The life and death part might come later.

"Passenger blast shields are closed," she replied. "Stand by for boarding tunnel deployment starting NOW."

He pulled the cover the rest of the way and dropped the rope. Seven meters drop to the top of the engine housing. Hopefully, nobody looking up right now as folks concentrated on their people returning.

Most of their people.

He watched the metal tube inch out under manual control.

Clunky. The automated system could do it just fine, but Rafferty was planning to look amateur here on purpose.

Noise and flash as a distraction.

He got close and Nafizul gripped his rope, sliding down quickly as the tunnel went thunk. He hung just overhead as it thunked a second time, then connected.

Dropping softly, he moved a meter to his right and located the space he wanted, right atop the stubby dorsal fin centered on the engine itself. The box Zadi had built got pulled out and he opened the top, flipping the power switch.

"Radio field test for telemetry," he said quietly.

"Picking up transmitter and locking in," Taggart replied. "Boarding has begun. You have about thirty seconds."

Hopefully time enough. The outer skin of the hull was a steel alloy with enough magnetism to hold. Plus the device would be turning it's own magnets on to an ultra-high level to anchor it.

He moved and found the spot Rafferty had pointed out. Aft of the air intakes where these engines could rotate from pure rocketry to skyjets by changing the fuel mix. Shielded somewhat from heat and airflow by the way the front of the engine pod flared larger, then tapered rearwards.

Box got set down. Thunked itself quietly in his hands, but that was magnets catching hold of hull.

"Telemetry read?" he asked.

"Contact solid and stable," she told him. "I have control of the device and activating secondary magnets now."

Nothing changed, but nothing was supposed to change. Nafizul waited for someone to pop up a turret and point it at him, demanding to know what the hell he thought he was doing.

"You're clear to depart," Taggart announced. "Tunnel will

detach in roughly ten seconds and I expect pre-flight to be somewhat abbreviated."

"Roger that," he replied.

Pity that they couldn't have turned down gravity in here, but it was enough that he was in vacuum at the moment. And strong enough to do this.

Hand over hand, he went back up the rope. That had been one of the things he'd done to rehab his arms while his leg healed enough for weight. Pull yourself up a rope with a ratchet holding your harness since you couldn't wrap your legs around the cord.

Later, he'd dropped the harness and climbed free. Nafizul had considered asking the Captain if he could install some sort of rock-climbing wall on the ship, but this bay was about the only spot with sufficient vertical clearance, other than the engine rooms.

Maybe later.

He got up quickly and into the access tunnel, slipping the missing panel back into place and setting the bolts by hand for now. Rafferty had said nothing more was needed, because he'd send someone in later to confirm all the work anyway, after repressurizing the entire bay.

"Radio, I'm clear here," he said, already feeling vibrations in his feet that must be the shuttle's engines lifting off.

"Vehicle has begun to depart the vessel," Taggart said. "We'll be sealing up the outer bay doors in thirty seconds and starting to pump in air. You have about fifteen minutes unless you needed to move faster?"

"I'll be coming out via that access airlock the Air Boss rigged," he replied. "We're only starting into trouble at this moment."

"Roger that," she replied. "I'll let him know and see you shortly."

Because his primary job on this ship was Gunnery Officer, with only occasional forays into espionage work. At least he hoped so.

Time to get to work.

33

———————

Padraig had moved to the bridge, bringing Torray and Cayne with him for now and putting Trinh to watch them. Farrell arrived after the other guests left, possibly at a dead run from the flight deck, given her color and heavy breathing.

"Radio, status of the shuttle?" Padraig asked.

"They might have set the autopilot from how smooth they are descending, sir," Nyssa replied. "Comm gear still answering signals."

Gunner Haque arrived at that point, bumping Andrea Whelan to a secondary station as he took over, the only note that things had gone strange was that he was wearing a full space suit with the helmet faceplate retracted.

Nothing jumped out at them. No ships suddenly began to maneuver or launch missiles.

Just another day at the office.

"Sirs, in about thirty seconds, I should trigger the recording," Nyssa said, breaking up the quiet.

Padraig turned to Torray.

"Would you care to give the order, Soon-To-Be-Former Supreme Autocrat?" he asked.

Torray grinned like a kid in a candy store with a bronze ten ducat coin in his hand from the grandparents.

"Squire Taggart, could you please order yourself and your ship to immediately depart this system and never return?" he spoke up.

Nyssa made a production of pressing a button on her console. Torray's voice immediately filled the bridge in high dudgeon. Apparently, it had only taken three takes to get it all, which was pretty impressive.

"Attention, *A'Zedi* vessel *Marrakesh*, this is the Supreme Autocrat," he thundered. "Such insults will not be acceptable. Ambassador Ussher is declared *persona non grata* and ordered to immediately depart the system aboard your vessel. Further, *Marrakesh* is ordered out of *Traisan* space at best speed. You will depart within the hour. There will be no further warnings given."

Considering the tool she'd had Zadinul Haque build, most of this hemisphere heard that warning.

"Message ends," Nyssa said. "Monitoring the shuttle, but they're not saying anything beyond basic landing communications."

"Stay on them, Radio," Padraig replied. "Mister Torray, I would appreciate if you remained sharp to reply to any surprise messages from the palace or the fleets around here before we got into motion. Otherwise, I would ask you to wait quietly as we move to save your life."

That got through to the man. Someone might decide to to order the fleet after them anyway, possibly preempting such an order from the Supreme Autocrat. Possibly as part of someone like Pera decapitating the former government.

Ussher had been of the opinion that it would take the four troublemakers something like a day to take out the Mistress at Arms. From there, an armed wariness where all four were watching each other and mobilizing their own organizations to do something.

Idly, he wondered if any might take Cayne's out and just run. Torray had planned it over something like a year, Padraig was given to understand, but the others were all smart men. They ought to have fallback positions.

Or they were about to discover why they'd needed them.

Marshall Ussher joined them, sliding into a station next to Torray with a nod to Padraig.

"Helm, pretending that we've caught by surprise, bring the bow around and begin acceleration up and out at reasonable rotary thruster speeds," Padraig ordered. "Ghostdrives as soon as you have clearance from the planet and a clean sailing corridor. Then haul ass at the best speed you can hit as we run. Radio, I need scanners set to double conic arrays. Give me forward and aft equally, so we know what's in front of us and who might start chasing."

"How soon until someone might react and chase?" Haque asked.

Padraig turned to his three experts, seated on one side of the bridge.

"One of those Super-Cruisers should be paying attention, but they ought to have no warning to ramp up systems," Cayne replied. Equerry to the Household meant that she talked transport and fleets. "And have no orders to pursue, given that you have been ordered to leave. The Supreme Autocrat would give that order, or heads would roll. And he would have given it to me, so they have two positions to fill to send the hounds after you."

"I'm more concerned about someone setting a border squadron on us," Torray noted. "They can get a message via Aetherial Communications Array fast enough to route someone."

"I plan on maneuvering crazy once we get distance," Padraig offered. "This ship was once pursued by a *Wronlori* Leviathan and we got away. We have a few tricks up our sleeves."

"And Ghost-space!" Halloran called, mostly so everybody was certain. "Engineering, I'm gonna ride them hard."

"We're tuned back here, Helm," Ahearn replied. "Might have known this was coming. Six ought to be a solid cruising speed. I'll see how much I can tack on past that."

"Everything you've got," Halloran said.

"Captain Boru," Torray said, "while I appreciate that you are saving your lives as well as mine, how has your crew been able to react to this situation with such surety?"

Padraig turned to smile at the man.

"Mister Torray, I have such an exceptional crew that I occasionally get hate mail from my fellow captains who are jealous," he replied. Stretching it, a bit, because most of them had no idea what *Marrakesh* really did, but there had been comments in bars. "Marshal Ussher challenged us to give our best here. You're seeing it."

Ussher grinned, appreciating that he'd mostly watched, but happy to take that credit when it mattered.

"Now what?" Torray asked.

"Now, we run," Padraig replied.

34

———————

Nyssa had the Aetherial Scanners tuned. And had had folks specifically replace a couple of older ones before they failed, knowing that they might be needed shortly.

All equipment failed eventually, if you left them to themselves. Zadi's main job on paper was handling those scanners when they needed to be rebuilt in the machine shop. And he did that, too.

Zarah had gotten them up to Six Point Two and held it for a while, before falling back to Six Point Oh. Six light-years per hour. One hell of an amazing speed for an old Transport to manage. And they'd never gone above a Four on the way in, so hopefully the folks behind them didn't know any better.

Nafizul had been of the opinion that the Super-Cruiser *Crimson Firebird* could hit Seven or a little higher. More than enough to run down most ships in this size category. Except where *Marrakesh* had enough of a running start.

Hopefully, they did.

"Helm, go ahead and initiate your next twist," Captain announced.

129

They were three hours out from Zulou. About sixteen light-years, given the time to accelerate after hitting Ghost-space.

"Adjusting flight path, aye," Zarah replied.

Nyssa was echoing the woman's console, so she could keep rear scanners aimed at the capital. They were already well past the range that any ship departing now would have been able to scan them, so if they launched on Zarah's initial course, they were more than fifteen degrees off.

But Nyssa also understood that there were scanner buoys everywhere, tracking ships like this for exactly this reason. *Crimson Firebird* would have to find one, drop out, query it, then jump back up to give chase, losing precious minutes every time they did.

Hard to run *Marrakesh* down doing that.

She turned to Captain Boru, rotating to her right to include the three visitors in the conversation.

"Sir, would they send a squadron of smaller ships after us instead of a Super-Cruiser?" she asked.

Marshal Ussher grew pensive. The two civilians were a little lost.

"They might, depending on how long it took for them to rearrange Jensen, Radio," Captain replied. "Keep watch anyway aft. I'm more concerned that someone might see that logic ahead of us and route down a raiding force to intercept."

"But they can't do anything in Ghost-space, can they?" Equerry Cayne asked, surprised.

Nyssa didn't answer that.

You could. *Marrakesh* had, but Maddox had been on the guns that day, with everyone taking several shots to track how Ghost-space ebbed and flowed.

"They can," Marshal Ussher spoke up. "It can be be done,

but it takes luck and effort. You have to match the other vessel, then manage to score a hit with plasma cannons. Hard to do, but doing so disrupts the flight envelope of a starship and kicks them down into real space immediately, often with damage."

Or dead, if you got a lucky hit, as Maddox had. Assuming it had been luck.

35

Padraig had sent Chance to sleep for now, certain that they'd have down time while *Traisa* recovered from a political decapitation. The border was most of a day's journey at this speed, giving someone time if they moved fast enough on Zulou.

"Radio, how many scanners have tracked us in the last hour?" he asked.

Nyssa had mostly rested, sitting in her chair and sipping coffee with occasional biobreaks and snacks from the drawer under her console. But she'd said she was prepared to run a full day as well, and Bex Magorian was also sleeping.

"Seven, sir," she replied after triple-checking. Because she did. "Helm slotted us down into something of a dark corridor where they don't have many occupied worlds. Invading fleet would be seen, but one quiet ship might not be. We're not that quiet, and I presume that the next Supreme Autocrat looks at these logs and probably adds a couple of beacons."

"Are they transmitting or just recording?" he asked.

"Stand by."

Padraig nodded. Normally, they were passive, but he expected a couple might have been sent to an alert status that would call for help.

"None currently broadcasting, but...oh, shit. Hold that thought."

She ignored him and started typing furiously. The rest of the bridge picked up her energy and Padraig could smell the surge of adrenaline.

"Zulou has transmitted an alert, sirs," she said, head still down and skull gleaming. "*Marrakesh* identified by name. Vector of escape given, but they've missed one or more of our turns, because we're clear at the edge of the cone they're projecting. All available vessels and buoys to locate and detain. Destroy if necessary."

She looked back at him with eyes a little big.

"Guessing Pera took out the others, if the palace moved this quickly," Ussher spoke up. Normally, we'd have gotten to the border and been facing a stern chase if they wanted us. Boru, what do you need from us?

"Radio, have they announced a new Supreme Autocrat?" he asked.

"Negative, sir," she replied. "Arodd Torray issued that order. I'm reasonably confident it was an impostor, though."

Padraig caught the grin on the man's face when he heard that.

"Most assuredly, Radio Officer," he said. "Captain, can we run?"

"Yes," Padraig said. "Helm, if we're at the edge of their search zone, push us even further. Radio, adjust forward scans to pick up forces attempting to intercept and make sure Halloran is aware of them. Guns, you will prepare both sets of teams for Ghost-space interception."

Nafizul gulped, the nodded. Single hardest shot possible on a starship, but it could be done. And they would be firing back at anyone trying to chase them. Kick them out first.

"What do you need?" Ussher asked.

"We run," Padraig replied. "Hide as much as we can, but once we cross the border, we have better options. At this point, everyone is in a holding pattern. Mister Torray, Mistress Cayne, perhaps we should get you settled in the Courier pod for now? Nothing is likely to happen for a few hours."

"Certainly, Captain," Torray said, rising. "Tom can show us. And could you assign me Farrell for a time?"

"Farrell, sir?" Padraig asked.

"I have no intention of being taken alive, Captain Boru," Torray said darkly. "She may need execute me if the vessel is somehow captured. I want you and your crew aware of my intentions at that point."

Not a lot to say to that. Padraig caught Ussher's nod and rotated to lock eyes with Cam Farrell.

"You will place yourself under Marshal Ussher's direct orders, Security," he said bluntly. "Armed as necessary. Act accordingly."

Even someone as hard and professional as Cam Farrell could go a little white around the edges, but she rose and nodded.

"Sir, yes, sir," she said, falling in with the other three as they departed.

The highest stakes possible.

But Padraig wasn't bluffing today.

36

———

Tom got them to the Courier interrupting the cleaning crew.

"Standing orders, sir," the woman in charge said, the rest barely looking up. "Everything stripped and inspected. Cleaned. Prepared for new guests, as we don't trust the previous guests to have not left any surprises."

And Expert Sailor Haque, cousin to the Gunner, was walking around with a hand scanner, poking and prodding everything as well.

Lynch stepped in from a previously-unused lounge.

"If you folks would care to join me here?" she asked.

Tom led. A few pastries from earlier. Hot coffee. Wet bar, depending on your needs.

Tom poured a sippy cup of coffee and adulterated it. The others got themselves settled.

Farrell loomed, but that was her potentially facing one of those career moments where you were standing in a court martial for doing everything right. When senior flag officers like him judged you with the exact science of hindsight.

"Tom, is he good enough?" Arodd asked. "Are they?"

Tom turned to Lynch. Let her answer.

"They will move heaven and earth, Mister Torray," she replied. "As to whether it will be enough I cannot speak. How good are your people?"

Tom turned to Cayne. The Equerry was the one who communicated with the fleets. Relayed orders. Explained situations. Not a sailor, but she'd impressed him with the depth of what she'd picked up over a couple of decades as a bright civilian.

She turned to Arodd.

"So we assume Ana?" she asked.

"I can't see anybody else pulling it together that quickly," Arodd replied. "Unless there was a dark horse back there that everyone missed. If that person took out Ana, the shuttle might have been second on their list. Move fast. Consolidate power and issue orders."

"Destroy *Marrakesh*?" she asked.

"If they knew I wasn't on the shuttle, all their behavior makes perfect sense," Arodd replied. "Tom? Your thoughts?"

"You suspected that someone was about to jump you, Arodd," Tom reminded him. "That you had to move immediately if you were going to get out. I lean toward Ana Pera masterminding, but I don't think that matters all that much. We get you to safety. Life goes on."

"Except that Ana didn't hear all the parts about making this less than a lifetime job," Irelyn said. "She might be expecting that Arodd sends assassins after her, so even if we do escape, we can't get away from her."

"Oh, give me a year," Arodd laughed like a generator losing a bearing. Rough and grinding. "Wasn't planning on reciprocating, but I might not have any choice there."

"Arodd, you can't vanish if you won't disappear," Tom said, hearing how silly it sounded even as he said it.

"No, but I can post bounties for Ana," he smiled cruelly. "Put up a bond, to be paid on delivery of her head to a banker somewhere. The assassins will take it upon themselves, so I don't have to communicate with them. Save the once."

Not a lot Tom could say to that. If that woman was coming after Arodd, she was probably coming after him, too, so it was merely prudent at that point.

"Then we're back to the top," Irelyn noted. "Is Boru good enough to pull it off?"

"If he can't, nobody can," Farrell broke her silence.

Tom studied the woman. Like all Boru's people, sharp and professional. And that extra gear for days like this.

Hopefully, that would be enough.

37

Nyssa was watching everything on passives, and a few places with active scanners that might be seen, but she didn't have much choice. *Marrakesh* was deep inside *Traisan* space. Behind enemy lines, if a new Supreme Autocrat had already taken power and declared war on them.

So she saw the signal. Or rather, the cluster of signals. Three of them. Clear out at the edge of her scanner range, run to starboard and above them some.

"Radio, possible contact," she said, but it wasn't an alert level voice. "Captain, your screen three."

"Noted, Radio," Captain replied. "Good catch. Assuming normal warships in service, add ten percent sensitivity. How far out might they scan us?"

Because *Marrakesh* had sensors at least as good as any scout or Survey vessel in business these days.

She went ahead and added a sphere around the three. It didn't touch *Marrakesh* at present, but might if both stayed on their respective beams.

"Helm, up ten, yaw three-five-five," Captain ordered.

"Helm up and port, aye," Zarah replied. "Maintaining a shade over Six, sir."

"Radio, any way to identify them at this range?" Gunner asked.

Nyssa was about to retort politely, then caught herself.

Was there?

"Stand by," she announced, then started digging in.

Hmmmm. How would you?

Speed was one indicator. Cluster of three ships might be cruisers, but a trio of Escorts was more likely. *Traisa* built them heavier than *A'Zedi*, almost up to Frigates by tonnage in some instances.

Then one of them pinged her and Nyssa was reasonably certain that they'd been seen. She typed quickly, bringing up known hull configurations. Nyssa didn't need to know who it was. Merely what.

"One of those three looks to be a Scout Escort, sir," she announced. "*Traisan* fleet logic suggests the others are also Escorts, but I can't identify hull type at this range."

"The number of guns they mount and the type is usually the only giveaway, Radio," Captain replied. "Generally three particle cannon mounts of various throw-weights and two missile launchers. Pretty standard hull. Churn them out by the job lots."

She'd take his word for it, though she did have scans of several that had been in Zulou orbit with them. And all those agreed with his assessment and her notes from base.

She routed everything to Nafizul.

He'd need them.

38

Tom looked up as Captain Moneaux appeared at the hatch. She'd largely stayed out of the way of things, letting him handle Arodd while she'd originally been assigned here mostly to interface with the ship.

And they could have left her home, as good as Kaitlin Lynch and Boru handled things, but some things you do because you have a checklist and it is easier to run with it.

"Sir, if I might have a few minutes?" Yasmin asked, not entering the room.

He turned to the others.

"Go," Arodd called. "We shall be here when you return."

Tom followed her out and noted that she closed the hatch behind her, before leading him entirely out of the pod and back into the ship, where Sailor Haque was waiting.

"What do you have for me?" he asked the two of them.

Yasmin turned to Haque to explain.

"Scans when the passengers boarded, sir," Haque replied. "Because we had a chance to scan Cayne the first time, I had baselines for the second. Went over the other folks first, but mostly I was looking for signatures of electronics or threats of chemical and biological weapons.”

Tom nodded. Perfectly logical and they’d briefed him what they were planning.

“And?” he asked.

“Equerry Cayne is armed, sir,” Haque continued. “Small and readily concealable. Something roughly equivalent to our Type Three Personal Disruptor.”

Tom nodded at that. Flatten an egg out some and hold it in your palm, fired with the thumb. Short range weapon. Not a lot of shots.

Excellent if you needed to assassinate someone.

“Where is it hidden?” he asked.

Haque blushed. Dark.

“According to the scans I’ve reviewed, between her breasts in her bra, Tom,” Yasmin said instead. “Scans showed a lump, but didn’t react to metal or a powercell, though they might have missed it anyway, depending. Or shielded against those scans.”

“No, they would not have,” Haque challenged.

“So she hid something when she came aboard,” Tom said. “What does that tell us?”

“None of the others were armed, sir,” Haque replied. “Went back and specifically checked, once I saw what she’d done. Not entirely sure how she did it, but I’m confident enough that she did.”

“And nobody was expecting Torray to bolt,” Yasmin continued. “That much was obvious as I’ve watched them and gone back and reviewed the footage. He got a jump on everyone. Cayne might be up to something. I would suggest that it is in our interests to at least temporarily disarm her.

Possibly have Haque here subject her to a very pointed, short-range scan in case she had other surprises."

He studied the woman. Captain, but administration and possibly espionage side of the fleet, rather than Line Command. Sharp. And willing to take the blowback from this herself, from the way she was standing.

Bad Cop, so he could continue to be Good Cop.

"Haque, Moneaux needs a weapon," he said. "Where do we locate one?"

The sailor reached for the bag he had slung across his back and brought it around front. A standard issue Adjustable Disruptor in a holster emerged and the sailor handed it to Yasmin.

Yasmin hooked it to her belt and thigh, then drew the weapon and checked it.

"Fully charged and checked out of the armory to me this morning by Farrell," Haque offered. "Not that she was expecting anything, but she's always expecting something."

"Excellence does that," Tom reminded the man, watching him puff up a little. "Yasmin, follow me and keep things under control. Haque, I'll need you scanning at the end, but not until then."

"Aye, sir."

Tom returned to the pod, taking a breath and opening the lounge hatch, the other two trailing immediately behind him.

"Farrell, stand down, that is a direct order," he said, loud and clear so she understood, because the woman was already reacting to Yasmin's pistol.

"Sir?" Farrell asked anyway, but remained still.

Yasmin stepped fully into the room and centered her Disruptor on Cayne.

"Security found something and sent it up the chain," Tom

told her. "Mistress Cayne, I would greatly appreciate no sudden movements on your part."

Arodd had clenched, but held. Cayne had been caught off guard, which was good.

"What's going on, Marshal?" Arodd asked.

"She has a disruptor she forgot to mention to everyone," Tom replied. "Cayne, I'm going to remove it. Anything in there likely to bite or sting when I do?"

Cayne's face had gotten dark. But then, she knew where he was about to stick a hand and he didn't figure any woman would find that attractive.

"No," she said. "It can be drawn from the top or the bottom," she replied.

"Normally, I'd have you lift your shirt to get to it, but I'd rather you stayed perfectly still so Moneaux doesn't have to shoot you," Tom replied. "My orders were to get him to safety. That's been extended to you, but it can be removed again, depending."

As in, you could be dead shortly if you gave us a reason. Yasmin was ready. Farrell was still.

Cayne had her hands out to the sides. Tom approached at enough of angle that he wasn't in Yasmin's way, then stuck a hand down the front of Cayne's blouse, unfortunately rooting a bit until he could get inside her bra.

That deadly egg came out and he stepped back. Roughly equivalent of a Type Three. Matte black. Charged, if that red light was the powercell indicator.

"Haque?" Tom said, moving clear.

The sailor stepped right up to the woman and stuck his scanner in her face from maybe thirty centimeters away. Then scanned her from that range.

"Huh," he said. "Might also be a knife in her right shoe."

Haque stepped back and watched.

Tom let his scowl speak volumes.

"It was agreed that everyone coming aboard the ship would be unarmed, Mistress Cayne," he reminded her. "If you'll allow Haque to remove your shoes, I'll get you replacements from ship's stores. You'll both need fresh clothes anyway, though I'm certain that we can get a tailor involved quickly enough."

Arodd's face was pensive, but not angry. Intensely watching.

Cayne's glare might etch hull metal, but she slowly bent down and unlaced her boots, then kicked them far enough away to make a statement.

"Haque?" Tom asked.

The sailor picked the right one up, fiddled a bit, and was holding a knife that he handed over pommel first.

Flat. Ground down both edges to a rounded tip. No crossguard. Not a particularly useful fighting weapon, but excellent if you happened to be in the same room with someone asleep who might not wake up after you cut his throat. Maybe adapted from a throwing knife, but he'd have to ask Farrell.

She was probably expert on that topic, too.

"Tom, all things considered, I think I might prefer sleeping alone for now," Arodd announced in a voice better suited to ordering lunch. "At least until we sort out what Irelyn was about."

And Tom agreed.

"Farrell, take charge of Mistress Cayne," he turned and ordered the woman. "Get her into different clothing. Have the doctor run a basic medical exam, and bunk her in one of the spare officer's quarters on the ship. Locked down somewhere between a guest from a different nation and a threat to the vessel and crew. Yasmin, go with her, but Farrell is in charge. Mistress Cayne, it will be for the best if you acquiesced to a change in circumstances at the moment."

Cayne rose, still scowling, but not in a position to do anything about it. Not unless she wanted to be shot. Farrell wasn't one to mess around, and her Adjustable Disruptor was probably on a stun setting.

Probably.

"Haque," he said, handing the man the egg and letting him take care of it.

Quickly, it was the three of them.

"Now what?" Arodd asked.

39

———

Kaitlin had watched it all unfold, but she'd seen Farrell in action and was willing to bet that Cam could have taken *everybody* in the room if she'd had to.

"Arodd," she answered the question, "how close were Irelyn and this Ana Pera I've not met?"

Arodd leaned back and she watched his eyes. Processing. Remembering. Recategorizing.

Tom merely watched, but he was between tasks at the moment.

"What are you suggesting, Madam Lynch?" he replied.

"Kaitlin," she corrected him. "We're far less formal, and you are a guest traveling with us now, rather than a formal head of state being conveyed in dignity."

"That will take some getting used to, Kaitlin," he grinned. "I have been **Supreme** for too long. Almost feel like I should get a job as a dishwasher or something in the back of a restaurant, just to remember humility."

"We can assign you shifts in the wardroom here, if that

149

would make you feel better," Kaitlin matched his grin. "I suspect you aren't that good of a cook, though."

The man laughed. Bold and bright and finally smiling.

"No, I haven't had to cook anything in twenty-five years," he said.

Then he turned serious.

"As to Irelyn and Ana, what were you suggesting?"

"Someone moved quickly on Zulou," Kaitlin said. "We expected the foursome on the shuttle to need a day to take out the Mistress at Arms, then start falling on one another after that. Instead, it wasn't that many hours before an alert was sent out to capture or destroy us. And they issued that order under your name, so someone has taken pretty much complete control of the situation in your former palace. I can't imagine the four survivors working it out among themselves that quickly, so I lean towards your theory that Pera got the jump on them. Irelyn brought a gun and a knife, both concealed well enough that they might have gone entirely unnoticed until she drew them. If she suspected you were fleeing and wished to accompany you, I imagine it would have been far easier to acquire a weapon on Bharani Prime if she was planning to kill you and steal all the money you'd hidden. This smacks of her moving preemptively, at the same time someone else was."

"Ana or that dark horse, in a personal conspiracy with Irelyn?" Arodd asked.

Kaitlin nodded.

"Anything might be possible," Arodd replied. Kaitlin could see the anger burning underneath the calm facade. "And I have no way of guessing what promises might have been exchanged in order to trigger this behavior. At this point, I'm simply glad that I jumped and ran when I did, as I get the feeling that I might have already been dead by now had I stayed at home."

"And we're glad to host you, Arodd," Kaitlin acknowledged. "I will remind both of you gentlemen that since the orders to capture or destroy *Marrakesh* went out under Arodd's name, technically he still appears to be Supreme Autocrat."

Both men watched her, uncertain as to where she was going.

"And the technical implications, Kaitlin?" Tom finally asked.

"Arodd mentioned that we'd never know what deal Pera and Cayne had worked out," she replied. "That's not entirely true. You could ask her. Interrogate her. Threaten her, even, as *Traisa* appears to have declared war on *Marrakesh* at least, if not *A'Zedi* by extension. That makes her an enemy officer. If you chose to interpret things that way."

Both men recoiled at her words, but Kaitlin wasn't surprised or offended. She generally tried to cultivate an image of a pleasant grandmother when strangers came aboard. Easier that way.

They didn't need to know she'd done thirty years in uniform could swear and brawl with the best of them.

Tom rose and made his way to the intercom, dialing a number.

"Bridge. Boru. Bit of a situation here."

"It's Tom Ussher. Have Farrell or Moneaux briefed you?"

"Only in the loosest terms, Marshal," Boru replied. "Cayne taken prisoner and disarmed. Removed from the pod."

"Yes, Captain," Tom said. "When your situation is resolved, we can provide more detail, but it may be necessary to treat Cayne like an enemy combatant. Normally not a problem, but this is your vessel."

"And we're in the process of being intercepted by a *Traisan* squadron, sir," Boru replied. "Not sure if we can run or fight them off. Contact in roughly ninety minutes at the current rate of closure."

"I'll leave that to you, Captain," Tom said. "Out."

Kaitlin watched him nod and return to sit.

"You heard."

"I did," Arodd replied. "It does not fill me with joy, but I knew that everything was a risk from the moment I got out of bed this morning. Does anything change?"

"Unlikely, gentlemen," Kaitlin interjected. "We can get a projection going here so you can follow what happens. The Courier Pod has a small flag bridge specifically for monitoring or commanding fleet actions."

"Let's do that, Kaitlin," Tom said, rising again. "I'd like to see how good Boru and his people are."

"Hopefully, they can surprise you, Tom."

40

Padraig studied the plot. Definitely trouble inbound, as the three had turned and begun an intercept course.

You could talk in Ghost-space. Aetherial transmitters sent their signal at very high FTL speeds, so it was something akin to normal radio wave propagation. Sensors worked the same way, which was how that scout had seen them.

Speed of closure suggested Escorts. Smaller ships, but three of them could overwhelm *Marrakesh* even then, as they were designed to tackle Frigates and Cruisers.

And running, while good, distinctly limited his firepower, even as every light-year he tacked on behind him was that much closer to escaping. You could use plasma cannons up there, if you got close enough, but not missiles.

"Gunner, I need up-to-date specs on *Traisan* Escort hulls," he said.

"Your screen four, sir," Haque replied a moment later.

Padraig studied them. Assault, Tactical, Scout, and Police Escorts, from most firepower to least.

If they had any size cruiser in there, *Marrakesh* was dead

meat, because even with the Escort Pod on back, they only now had something like Light Cruiser firepower to work with, so he went ahead and assumed small ships. That was normal for *Traisa* anyway.

Of greater concern was that the Scout might have gotten a message back to Zulou, and someone like *Crimson Firebird* was coming. And fast enough to run them down if he had to evade more trouble.

"Gunner, we're going to have to go for broke," Padraig announced. "Helm, when they get close, I want you to turn into them without slowing. Plot a course that passes below them at high speed, then turns away again and returns to best flight vector to escape."

"Sir?" Halloran asked.

"I want them to have to stop and circle back, instead of being able to sidle right up behind us the first time and try to knock us out of Ghost-space, Helm," Padraig explained. "Then I want a stern chase in Ghost-space for as long as we can manage it."

"Sir, yes, sir."

Padraig nodded and turned his attention to Nafizul. Man had good ratings and a good crew, but the Escort Pod would be a bit of a wildcard and Haque hadn't taken this ship into battle even for a training mission, so he might be a little rusty.

"Gunner, I have no idea if it is possible or not to achieve, but I want you to program all of the turrets to fire on a specific vector, with every weapon parallel as a hose," Padraig said. "Work with Radio to set them to all fire simultaneously, with her providing the actual moment to pull the trigger. Questions?"

"I have three prospective targets, Captain," Nafizul replied. "Which one should I go after?"

"Good question," Padraig acknowledged. "Radio, we presume one Scout in that mess?"

"Aye, sir."

"Look at their flight characteristics and see if there is any way to guess which one might be what," he ordered. "Tactical Escort hull has better squadron command spaces and might be the squadron leader. Assault has better guns and weapons. I'd prefer the Tactical if you can identify them. Gunner, if not, skip the Scout and hammer one of the others."

"Aye, sir."

Padraig leaned back and watched them close.

Hopefully, he could pull a surprise here, because they should be expecting the last of the old M-boats still in service, and didn't realize that *Marrakesh* was probably one of the most combat-experienced warships in the fleet today.

Maybe he could give them a proper introduction shortly.

41

———

Nafizul sent a detailed note to Armiger Aisha Takach, Gunnery Officer off the Escort Pod.

Her reply consisted of nine question marks in a row, which made him feel better, so he opened a line.

"Sir?" she asked.

"One hard broadside salvo in Ghost-space, sailor," he replied, trying to sound like a guy who got weirder shit in his breakfast cereal box.

Maddox Nevin had cast a long shadow on this crew. *Murderhobo* hadn't been able to live up to it. Nafizul was going to try.

"Can we hit anything at that rate of closure, Knight?" she countered.

He glanced over at Nyssa Taggart. Her calm smile made him more confident.

"We'll be on a beam, Takach," Nafizul replied. "Assuming that they hold their speed, we can predict it. If they catch on to what we're doing and slow, Radio should be able to calculate that. The shot will be automatic on signals from her console.

All we're doing is setting it up, then taking individual charge of the guns after she's done."

"Got it, sir," Takach said. "All four turrets forward, with elevation preset, followed by presumed rotation aft."

"Correct, Armiger," Nafizul said. "Make sure you have all of your generators and cooling systems on, because I fully intend you to go for a shitshow if we drop out of Ghost-space when this happens. Three enemy vessels, but we'll be trying to kill them sequentially, starting with the toughest one."

"We've got you covered, sir."

Nafizul cut the line and turned to Radio.

"We can do this, right?"

42

Nyssa missed Maddox, but Nafizul was turning out to be a pretty cool dude. Listened to Squires, two ranks below him on the scale, and sold his people. Even if he wasn't as certain.

"Affirmative, Nafizul," she said quietly. "Rate of closure right now would be Thirteen and change, but they might back that off when Zarah turns and charges them. We'll have the guns at twenty degrees elevation for the longest possible crossing on their vector. I'm identifying Number Two as your target for this, and making sure that we stay on him."

"Radio, would it be easier to keep all the guns nailed in place and me flare as needed?" Zarah asked.

"Can you react fast enough?" Nyssa asked.

"Probably not, but I can program the system to keep the bow on them as we close. Assuming we stay below them on the intercept vector, the gyroscopes can swing the ass around faster than friction in Ghost-space can actual effect a turn. That's what you needed, right?"

Nyssa considered it. Went ahead and turned back to Captain Boru, because he'd just been sitting there listening to the three of them work instead of issuing orders or asking questions.

Like he knew she could do it.

Captain Boru nodded once.

So maybe she could. Heady concept.

"Helm, do that," Nyssa ordered. *ORDERED.* "Gunner, set all plasma cannons on a spread no wider than ten degrees horizontal, centered forward. Elevation twenty degrees and locked in. Firing command will be automated and triggered by my sensors when enemy vessels are predicted to be in range."

She paused there, head down trying to remember what she'd missed.

"Excellent work, Radio," Captain said. "Engineering, we're going to pull a jousting pass shortly. All hands stand by for Damage Control operations."

Nyssa nodded and went back to her boards. There would be some complicated math involved in handling all this.

Good thing they had upgraded her console to handle cryptography, which was two orders of magnitude messier.

43

———

Padraig didn't have much to do at this point. His people had set out a plan that he'd approved by not overriding them. But they were operating as a team, even with a new player facing his first space battle.

Padraig, having see how many gun battles Haque had been in on the ground somewhere, was less worried than he might have been. That man knew how to kill people.

"Radio, call the countdown," he said simply.

"Estimated time to contact forty seconds," Nyssa replied. "All vessels maintaining vector. Okay, I'm starting to get a flare from the squadron, but not well coordinated."

Not impossible to do at these speeds, but exceptionally complicated and not something most squadrons would have practiced.

How often was someone charging you in Ghost-space after all?

"Helm, I've got them," Halloran called. "They are slowing and preparing to turn for a pursuit. Just as predicted, if a little

161

early. They will be able to give chase pretty quickly when we blow by."

Much harder to turn like that in real space, where you had to use the rotary thrusters to do things. Ghost-space was more like being on water than anything. Not as solid a base to push against as land, but not vacuum, either.

"Gunner, after your shot, rotate everything aft," Padraig ordered. "Radio, maintain watch on our forward vector, as well as keeping an eye lateral back to Zulou, just in case."

Nothing showing on the boards right now, but Padraig would have been deeply surprised if they hadn't sent a Super-Cruiser off at full speed to run *Marrakesh* down.

It's what he would have done, and he had to presume his enemy was at least somewhat competent, if not particularly expert.

They might not be three meters tall, but never assume they are only one, either.

"Target is on our port as we close," Nyssa said.

"I got him," Halloran replied. "Gunner, stand by as I think I'll centerline him just right."

Padraig had to agree. Zarah Halloran was making it look easy, when he knew how complicated things like this were. At the same time, she'd done it before. And had a natural gift for maneuver that had gotten her assigned to *Marrakesh* immediately out of school, instead of a smaller vessel somewhere.

Good thing for him.

"Five seconds to intercept," Nyssa called.

Nafizul had actually taken his hands and put them in his lap, which Padraig found surprising and welcome. He trusted the Squire beside him to pull it off and was willing to let her.

"Intercept," Nyssa said simply. "Scanning now. Gunner, you are free to engage."

"Helm, give me a random vector now," Padraig ordered. "Something to throw off their calculations and buy us an extra five seconds."

Her shoulders flexed, then Halloran started typing.

"Radio, I'm only seeing two signals in Ghost-space," Padraig called, looking at his boards. "Confirm that."

"Confirmed, sir," she replied a moment later. "Target appears to have been forced out."

Welcome news, because they might be fifteen or thirty minutes recovering, depending on what had happened and how well that crew could react.

The books said that the plasma channel triggered massive short circuits that tripped breakers everywhere. If the right ones went, the ship was dead in space until Damage Control teams could get to them and do a manual reset.

And sometimes, you put a shot somewhere that did extra damage that had to be repaired. Civilian freighters might suffer catastrophic failures, as has happened that one time at Varfelis Station, but Padraig assumed warships in service here.

But time was time, and twenty minutes was two light-years distance to make up at these speeds.

"Enemy comm signals intercepted," Nyssa said. "They confirm *Marrakesh* intercept and are calling for help. Sent in clear text because they were in a hurry, but they might receive a reply encoded, depending."

"Helm, keep us running for that gap," Padraig said. "Gunner, you'll order Helm make adjustments to engage enemy vessels over-the-shoulder from Ghost-space. Do not ask me for permission, because that will only slow us down. Am I clear?"

"Sir, yes, sir," Nafizul replied automatically.

Padraig wanted the man on autopilot. Letting muscle memory handle things so he didn't overthink it.

Just aim and fire, then try to guess how eddies and tides in Ghost-space twisted your shot before adjusting and trying again. Maddox had had a preternatural instinct for it. Padraig had no idea how good Nafizul would be.

On-the-job-training day.

"Two enemy vessels have come about and are beginning to accelerate in our wake," Nyssa announced.

"Identify them for tonnage based on speed they can achieve closing," Padraig replied.

Super-Cruisers would max around Seven, depending. Escorts ought to be able to reach Eight Point Five for short bursts.

Marrakesh was running all out at Six, so they knew what they needed to do to catch him.

If they could.

44

Tom had taken the communications station in the Courier's flag bridge and still remembered most of the old tricks. He was echoing Boru's readout on passive, with the intercom listening in but muted, so he didn't get in their way.

Kaitlin was in the admiral's chair and Arodd stood next to her. Farrell had returned and taken a spot in the corner. Yasmin was next to Tom typing occasionally but hardly speaking. She hardly spoke most of the time.

"What just happened?" Arodd asked.

Tom had to remind himself that the man was a politician and not a sailor. Cayne would have probably seen it.

"Boru managed one of those lucky shots that damaged one of the three enemy vessels," Tom said.

"That man manufactures his luck," Arodd replied flatly.

"Not disputing you," Tom replied, having watched what a sharp crew could do when well trained and well commanded. "From here, we're running again. I presume shooting at each other when they get close enough, because if they just sit back, we might escape."

"Are they the hounds for the hunter, Tom?" Kaitlin asked. "Just marking us for someone else?"

He paused and considered that.

"*Crimson Firebird*," he said, turning to Arodd. "How good a shape was it in, if suddenly ordered to haul ass to run us down?"

Arodd's mouth pinched sideways.

"That design was intended to chase down Heavy Cruisers and outrun Ships of the Line," he mused. "They'd just come in from the border with you and should have been ready for a pursuit, but we also jumped and possibly caught them in the middle of something else. Plus, the Supreme Autocrat who ordered them in pursuit might have been me. Do we drop out and order them to return to base if they show up?"

"Hold that thought," Tom said.

He opened a line forward and asked Boru for a moment of his time.

"Kinda busy at this juncture," Boru said a moment later on the comm.

"Understood, Captain," Tom replied. "Arodd wonders if we might drop out and order that squadron to return to base, since nobody has announced a new Supreme Autocrat and he ordered them after us in the first place. Colossal bluff, but it might work. Hell, we might have him tear a strip of flesh off someone's ass and order them to escort us."

He watched Boru chew on that.

"They might be a little wound up at the moment, Marshal," Boru offered.

"And they might be a little uncertain how you did that," Tom chuckled. "I'd be second-guessing, if I didn't know. Risky, I know, because that third one can probably catch up again if we do."

"Captain, this is Arodd Torray. I am happy to run such a bluff, if you think it would work here. Or not, but I am given to understand that we cannot actually outrun trouble at this point?"

Tom listened to the sound at that end get muted. Changed the ambient noise on the signal. Then Boru was back.

"You are correct," Boru said. "They are closing at about an Eight, so they will overhaul us shortly. The third ship will be some time, and we don't know who else might be coming. Mister Torray, if you and Kaitlin could swap places, the cameras on the admiral's station were designed to make someone look impressive. We'll drop and see what we can do. If nothing else, we have enough short-range firepower to deal with two of the three Escorts."

Tom nodded. Hold them off and bluff them, worrying all the while about a Super-Cruiser coming up from behind and gunning for them hard.

"As with you and *Marrakesh*, I intend to manufacture some luck today, Captain," Arodd said. "Thank you."

"Thank me when we get you to safety, sir."

Tom cut the line and leaned back.

This was where it got tricky.

45

Padraig took as deep a breath as he could, then released it after a four-count.

"Helm, stand by to drop us out of Ghost-space," he ordered. "Engineering, we might not be staying long. Gunner, full defensive posture, engaging any incoming threats. Radio, maintain a full sphere scan against trouble sneaking up on us."

Bodies flinched and worked.

"Helm, drop us out."

And back to the real universe, instead of Ghost-space. Middle of nowhere, some two and a half light-years from the nearest major star, but they were in a spot without a lot of junk, either. No brown or red dwarfs around here. Not a lot of anything.

Good place to try to do something this amazingly crazy.

"Two vessels have overshot and are turning now," Nyssa called. "They were not prepared and are ragged in maneuvers. Third vessel has just gone to Ghost-space and is closing. We may end up bracketed in real space, depending."

Padraig had expected that. Two in front of him, relative to the border. One might end up behind him if they were sharp.

Bad place for Escorts, though, as they worked best when all three could protect one another. *Marrakesh* still outgunned a Tactical Escort by a reasonable amount.

"Stand by for Group One to emerge," Nyssa called. "Ten seconds or so."

"Supreme Autocrat, you will be cut into the circuit when they arrive," Padraig said, connecting the bridge lines to the flag bridge aft.

"Standing by, Captain," Torray replied.

"Contact," Nyssa called. "Confirm one Scout and one Tactical Escort in close formation."

Padraig couldn't help the grin. That probably meant that they'd hit the Assault Escort with that volley.

"*Traisan* vessel *Kyushu* hailing," Nyssa said. "Tactical."

Padraig leaned back and hoped that Arodd Torray could pull this one off.

46

———

Arodd Torray had carved his way to supremacy over a small pile of bodies.

Then added to the pile later, when others thought that they should be at the top of the stack instead.

He'd happily added them to the stack himself in some cases.

A woman appeared on the screen in front of him. Escort Commander Rank. Early thirties.

Arodd had his camera on and could see an echo of his image as he watched her.

Boru was right, those cameras made him look ten years younger and a lot healthier.

Useful.

"Escort Commander, I am the Supreme Autocrat," he announced in a voice he'd heard called an angry drawl. "What do you think you are doing?"

She blinked rapidly, suddenly gone from prepared to aggressively demand his surrender to possibly facing her worst possible nightmare as a commanding officer.

She fell back on professionalism, which was really what he demanded out of the fleet.

"Sir, we were issued orders to intercept the vessel *Marrakesh*," she said. "Stand them down or engage them if they would not heave to."

"We have heaved to, Escort Commander," he continued. "Whoever issued those orders did so in error, as I was in the process of taking a tour in this vessel and preparing to visit the station at Grandingham. You will stand down. You will order *Kyushu* to stand down. When the third vessel arrives, you will order it to stand down. In fact, your squadron will escort us to Grandingham."

Her mouth opened and closed just as sharply.

"Yes, Escort Commander?" he invited her to speak.

Not always the smartest move when addressing a Supreme Autocrat, but he would give the woman credit for doing everything with professional aggression. Like she was supposed to.

"*Marrakesh* fired on us, sir," she said carefully.

"You approached us like pirates, Escort Commander," he retaliated mildly. "I'm just glad that it wasn't necessary to order all three of you destroyed. Unless you felt the need to challenge my orders now?"

In political duels, that phrase was usually the first step in a dance that left another body on a pile somewhere.

You only challenged the Supreme Autocrat when you were planning to replace him yourself.

"Supreme Autocrat, this is Radio Officer Taggart. Vessel *Gauntlet* has just arrived in system. It is currently on a rear flank with *Kyushu* and *Arkwright* ahead."

"Excellent work, Taggart. Escort Commander, what is your name?"

"Luísa Cabral, Supreme Autocrat."

"Cabral, are you ordering *Gauntlet* to stand down, or do I need to destroy all three of you as pirates?"

"Stand by, sir."

Arodd found the button to freeze things at his end, camera turning gray and banded with mute function activated.

"Arodd, **I** might be surrendering," Tom Ussher noted with a light tone. "Truly impressive."

"Supreme Autocracy exists in their minds more than anything," Arodd told him. "Whoever replaced me fucked up by not immediately overthrowing me publicly. If that buys us the hours and light-years we need, I'm happy to take advantage of it."

The screen came live again, showing Cabral.

"Supreme Autocrat, *Gauntlet* has acknowledged new orders," she said precisely. "What course should we lay in?"

"Radio Officer Taggart, you will work with the squadron to get us in motion again," he said tiredly. "One preferably with fewer interruptions."

"Aye, Supreme Autocrat," the woman said. "Contacting them now on a direct line."

Arodd cut this line and sighed.

"Shit, I had forgotten how heavy that job is, and I've only been away from it for a few hours," he told the others. "I am so looking forward to a vacation for the first time in over a decade."

"We'll get you there, sir," Tom said.

Arodd hoped so.

47

Nafizul studied the scan results Nyssa had laid out for him. Scout. Tactical. Assault.

Someone had scorched the paint on the Assault Escort pretty good. Might be appropriate to apologize later.

And maybe not. The Supreme Autocrat had called them pirates.

All three hull designs had three weapon mounts on bow and wings, with two missile tubes on the nose. Assault had a Heavy Particle Cannon centered. Scout had special sensors instead.

All combined, he was looking at seven Particle Cannon mounts, plus a heavy. Throw in six missile launchers and they had a little better firepower than *Marrakesh* did, but spread out on three hulls, so fragile.

A duel would have been messy. And just about evenly matched, save that he was on a veteran warship and they'd shown themselves to be only pretty good. The *Traisan* squadron would have been a little twitchy after flying into a Ghost-space salvo.

And that was before somebody dropped a Supreme Autocrat on them.

Nyssa turned to look at him.

"Where do you want our escorts, Knight?" she asked in a formal kind of voice.

Normally, that was the Captain's decision, but she wasn't asking a political question.

Tactical one.

"Put the Leader directly on our bow, leading us to… Grandingham?" he asked.

"Grandingham, yes," she said. "Border station and fleet base. Not the main one, but the closest on this vector."

"Okay, all three in front of us like fingers," Nafizul replied. "Honor guard and that sort of thing, flying escort for the Supreme Autocrat in case some dumbass pirate comes along."

Nafizul waited for the captain to override him, the Boru didn't, so this might be the right call. Not that it mattered that much in Ghost-space, because there would be a gap too wide to shoot across, but it would look good on your long-range scanners.

He listened to her transmit sailing orders to the other ships, then the augmented squadron was in motion again.

Abruptly, she closed down most of her console and slid out as Bex Magorian took her place. Nafizul hadn't worked with Magorian that much. Small and slight. Strawberry blonde with freckles that reminded him of a lot of the folks he'd encountered in *Traisa* on operations.

Nafizul's overall coloration tended to work against him in undercover operations, but there were usually deep-cover folks for that. He'd spent more time as an assassin and troubleshooter than anything so it hadn't mattered.

He was still a troubleshooter. Hopefully, they'd done all the shooting they needed today.

Nyssa went aft to the pod to talk to the Supreme Autocrat directly with Captain Boru's approval. She found the group in the flag bridge section, four plus Cam.

"Ah, Radio Officer Taggart," Torray said as she entered. "How may I assist you?"

She had to stop and focus, because it was almost like a stranger had taken over his skin, all warm and friendly instead of grim and intimidating like he'd been when he first boarded.

"Grandingham, sir," she replied, taking up the flag communications station and bringing it live. "We've altered our course to put us on a more direct approach, rather than skirting it at high speed as originally intended. What do we need to prepare for on arrival?"

"A colossal bluff, Taggart," Torray replied evenly. "I'm still Supreme Autocrat because someone fucked up and didn't depose me already. As a result those people will be falling all over themselves at a surprise inspection by a foreign warship and myself. Then we'll order them to stand down and sail happily away. At least that's my current fantasy. What might you have to destroy such a dream?"

His smile was jarring, compared to his words, but the man was relaxed.

Free?

Nyssa understood that she'd lived far too sheltered a life, both before enlisting and since, happy to wallow in her data and encryption systems. What was it like to suddenly escape a death sentence? Even on in a gilded cage?

"We didn't sail close to Grandingham on the way in, so I don't know what fleet elements they might have in harbor, sir," she replied, staying short and professional. "Nor how easily we might bluff them out the back. I presume that you will need to publicly resign at some point so they don't automatically presume we've kidnapped you?"

"Something like that, yes," he told her. "I'm surprised that whoever it was didn't send that type of alert, now that you mention such a scenario, but I will not look such a gift horse in the mouth, as it were."

He paused and turned to the Marshal.

"Tom, is there any way to send a note to your people such that a *Directorate* squadron might meet us somewhere as an escort?"

"As soon as we know where we're emerging, I had intended to," Ussher replied. "Anything I send now is likely to be detected by someone in front of us. There is a risk that they can decrypt it."

"No, sir," Nyssa corrected the man. "I have access to signals processing codes that are currently unbroken as of last report from home. They will not be able to crack it that quickly. Later, perhaps. After we're safe. Not today."

He scowled at her, then relented when he remembered the bits he was allowed to know.

The Supreme Autocrat watched the byplay.

"If you are that certain, I would appreciate more escorts when we get to neutral space, Tom," he said.

The Marshal relented.

"Radio, I'll write up a message for you to encode and transmit," he accepted. "They are likely no more prepared to intervene than *Traisa* was to react, as Arodd moved faster than I expected. They are, however, poised and awaiting your signal. Arodd, they will not violate your economic zone, so there are limits to what they can do. We'll have to get to them."

Nyssa started to say something when the intercom chirped.

"RADIO!" Bex announced. "CONTACT!"

Nyssa was already running for the bridge.

49

Padraig had wondered how long he had until his luck finally ran out. It had been one hell of a run to this point, but karma could be a bitch when it finally bit you.

"Bex, what do you have?" he said, locked in hard on his screens as she typed furiously.

"Single signal, sir," she replied. "Traveling at a little over Mark Seven at present. Maybe Seven Point Three, but that's wavering. Inbound Vector puts them not far off a direct line back to Zulou."

"Presume that Super-Cruiser, Magorian," he told her. "Route all data to Haque and make sure nobody else can sneak up on us."

"Roger that, sir," she said.

Padraig dialed a line aft.

"Flag bridge. Ussher."

"Marshal, we have a single vessel closing at high speed," Padraig said. "Circumstances suggest a *Traisan* Super-Cruiser on intercept, but we won't know until we engage. They can outrun us and will overtake before we can get to Grandingham.”

“Understood, Boru,” the Marshal replied. “Stand by.”

“Boru, what are our options?” Torray asked.

Padraig grimaced. Bad and worse, but they knew that already.

“If we let them run us down, they can do the same thing to us that we did to the Escort, sir,” Padraig offered. “I listened to your bluff of the Escort squadron. Assuming someone else coming up behind us from the capital, would they fall for it?”

“Unlikely, Captain,” the Supreme Autocrat replied. “Someone coming from Zulou likely knows the full truth.”

“Arodd, would your replacement be aboard that vessel?” Marshal Ussher asked.

There was a long pause.

“All things considered, Captain Boru, I would rate those odds at better than even,” Torray replied.

“Can we bluff the Escorts into doing their usual job if things get political?” Padraig asked. “If we picked a battlefield and let that cruiser come to us?”

“Fight it out anyway?” Torray asked.

“*Traisan* Super-Cruiser, sir,” Padraig replied. “Generally a rough equivalent to an *A'Zedi* Battle Cruiser. Significant firepower, but they sacrifice armor and internal bracing for speed and guns. Fragile, if you will. If we let them run us down, we’re dead, simple as that. I’d like to even the odds some.”

Another pause, but Padraig understood that they were rolling the dice here. But then, the Supreme Autocrat had accused him of making his own luck.

Sometimes, that meant forcing the issue on your terms.

Padraig was happy with that idea today.

“Captain Boru, when you contact the Escorts, tell them

that you have been appointed Fleet Commander by the Supreme Autocrat," Torray said. "I'd get you a new uniform for it if I could, but they'll believe it or they won't. Take charge of the force and fight it as you see fit. Questions?"

"Sir, no, sir," Padraig replied and cut the line.

If nothing else, that would sure as hell look interesting in his personnel file, though he wondered how legal it was. Save that whoever had done the deed on Zulou hadn't removed Arodd Torray from power, so he was still officially the Supreme Autocrat of the *Enlightened Tyranny of Traisa*.

He shrugged.

Taggart entered at that moment.

"Magorian, change stations but remain on the bridge," he ordered. "Contact the other three vessels and inform them of my promotion by the Supreme Autocrat. Tell them to stand by for orders. Taggart, we're going to fight. Find me a nice, open arena where we have space to play, then make sure the Gunner approves. Let's go, people."

Serious risk, but it was the navy, and nobody ever promised you that you would die in bed.

50

Marrakesh had run on a distance, but Padraig had dropped them out far enough in the middle of nowhere that there were no inhabited worlds nearby watching.

Last thing he needed was a fleet arriving from Grandingham to investigate strange scanner readings when this might be a duel for the future of the *Enlightened Tyranny of Traisa*.

If he could pull it off.

"Gunner, you'll be coordinating fire," he reminded Nafizul. "What do you need?"

"Likely, this will be a combined arms exercise, Captain," Nafizul replied. "They have significant Heavy Particle Cannon broadside, but only eight missile tubes total to our ten. Similarly, they don't really have a lot of defensive firepower, because that design was intended to sit in the same position we are. That is, behind a line of escorts. If they can maneuver to stay clear of our missiles, they will be able to hammer us with long-range fire. We either have to remain outside of that range and duel with them, or close aggressively and attempt to overwhelm them. Costs would normally be prohibitive, but I understand that our options are limited."

"Let's ignore windage calculations then, Haque," Padraig told him. "We'll go for the throat. Radio, stack all four of us vertically and at rest. The Scout *Arkwright* just above us. The Assault Gauntlet above that. *Kyushu* topmost. A cunning captain might try to run a little long and drop behind us, rather than just sliding in on our bow, so tell them to expect to use their gyroscopes immediately on contact, with an expectation of a charge inward firing. Remind them that the enemy warship is a pirate and we're transporting the Supreme Autocrat of the *Enlightened Tyranny of Traisa* today."

"Roger that, sir," Nyssa replied.

Padraig leaned back and watched that signal close rapidly now that his squadron had dropped into real space and was taking up a defensive position.

Not just a colossal bluff, because any one of those other three might decide to switch sides at any moment and fire into *Marrakesh*. If he had all three supporting him, Padraig figured that he had an even chance of pulling this off. Without any of them, he was likely a prisoner of war. Tom Ussher might be executed as a spy, depending.

Arodd Torray was dead meat.

"Radio, call the cadence," he ordered.

"Estimated contact in twenty seconds," Nyssa replied. "They were at a bit of distance when we emerged, so they might not have our exact coordinates. Expect some maneuvering as they arrive."

"Helm, make sure you relay all maneuver orders through Radio for the squadron," Padraig ordered.

"Boru, it's Ussher. I can handle squadron communications if you'd prefer. We're set up for it aft and I still remember how from my wet-behind-the-ears days. That leaves your people free to do their jobs."

Padraig had forgotten that there was an open line aft, because they'd been muted most of the time. And he had no idea how good Tom Ussher was, but just having him do that added both another set of hands and he had the Supreme Autocrat immediately at hand to reinforce things.

If it came to that.

"Do that, Ussher," Padraig ordered a superior officer, feeling a little weird doing so, but needs must when the devil drives. "Radio, bring the flag bridge into the circuit and take command of all squadron communications as Helm and Gunner need you."

Once upon a time, Nyssa Taggart would have flinched at such a thing. Scrunched down in on herself. Blushed to the top of her shaved-bald skull.

That was the old Nyssa.

"Aye, sir. Locking them in now."

That vessel got closer.

And closer.

"Radio. Contact. Vessel *Crimson Firebird* identified. Sir, they're hailing us."

"Main screen, Taggart," Padraig replied, checking the readout.

Still out a ways. Beyond effective missile range and well past the point where even Heavy Particle Cannons could focus.

A face appeared. Woman. Possibly in her late thirties or early forties. Lean, with a face like a hatchet. Light brown hair and hazel eyes. Padraig supposed some men might find her attractive. But then, there was someone for everyone.

The lack of a uniform in the image made her stand out.

"This is Captain Padraig Boru of the *A'Zedi* fleet," he

announced. "We are in route to Grandingham with the Supreme Autocrat aboard. Identify yourself and state your purpose."

"Good, I found you," she replied. Almost purred, but it wasn't a pleasant sound. "Mistress at Arms Ana Pera. I've come to kill the Supreme Autocrat. And the rest of you if you don't give him up immediately. Which will it be?"

Padraig was just about to tell the woman to get stuffed when Arodd Torray spoke up.

"Hello, Ana," the man said. "Decided to try your luck, have you?"

51

Arodd still sat in the fancy station that made him look even better than the cameras at home. If he was ever returning, it might be worth having a chat with his AV people.

Somehow, he'd known it would be her. And that she'd be aboard. That was why he'd give Boru permission to try a stunt this crazy. He was still the Supreme Autocrat, and even now she was playing by whatever informal rules existed in such a game.

Challenge him to a fight to the death. Granted, usually with knives or poison, but beggars can't be choosers, and he'd tried to run. To escape her.

To live free.

Because he would not live in fear. In that, he was utterly undaunted.

"I will kill you, Arodd," Ana announced.

A text scroll across the bottom of his screen caught his eye.

*** Making sure of our three Escorts by invoking your name and wrath. Same with Crimson Firebird. Quietly. Taggart ***

Arodd found a whole new layer of smile at those words.

That woman might be young, but she was dangerous enough that he would have assigned a whole team of Ana's people to keep watch on her. And he doubted that Ana believed such a thing was possible, but Arodd had spent enough time around Boru's people to appreciate that they'd been assigned here.

Someone on Horwin had really respected him to have sent such an exceptional crew on a mission this arcane and complex.

And them, like him, undaunted entirely.

"Ana, you are my Mistress At Arms," Arodd told her, playing for the galleries now, presuming that Taggart was making sure that *Crimson Firebird* heard these words, too. Regardless of what Ana might have told them.

She had made a critical mistake at the top by not assuming command herself. He was still the boss. At least on paper.

"I am the Supreme Autocrat of the *Enlightened Tyranny of Traisa*," he continued. "If you wish to dance, we shall. And I will add your body to the pile. Or you can chose exile at this moment. Turn around and run for some border station, then debark and disappear. I promise that I will let you go at that point. Maybe you can find something useful to do with your life."

"I will be the Supreme Autocrat, Arodd," she sneered. "Over your dead body."

"So be it," Arodd decided. "Captain Boru, the stage is yours."

52

———

Padraig had been listening as the signal to *Crimson Firebird* got cut. Nyssa had linked him in with all the things she was doing as well, routing information through Magorian and Ussher as she did all those little things that had gotten a young enlisted woman bumped up time and again.

One of these days, he was looking forward to visiting her first command, like he wanted to go see Maddox Nevin. It would be utterly glorious.

"Helm, engage as we planned," he ordered. "Radio, have our Scout get to work blinding them. Gunner, stand by to charge."

There was no way in hell to win an engagement with a Super-Cruiser at this range. They could sit back and snipe at him until they hit something important.

He would need to get right up in their faces and punch them.

The only question was who would break first, and how good a captain that woman had on what had become her flagship.

Time to find out.

53

Nafizul had already determined that he wouldn't be doing any aiming today. Not even pulling triggers, because he had four ships of different sizes and capabilities that he needed to coordinate.

Combat at this sort of extreme range on a planet's surface was usually a factor of windage, humidity, gravity, and geometry. Not a lot different here, save that Captain Boru had given him time to prepare the battlefield.

He was beginning to understand how Maddox Nevin had turned out to be so impressive on paper, because Boru listened to ideas, then refined them.

"Tyrant Squadron, this is Haque," he said on a line linking him to his own gunnery teams, the pod on his back, and three strangers that were possibly going to have second thoughts shortly. "All ships rotate on gyros and begin to accelerate. We will take them down our port-side hemisphere at high speed where our size and maneuverability work in our favor. Stand by to launch missiles on my command. All ships acknowledge and conform."

Jousting pass, because why the hell not? He had to get a lot closer for the bulk of his Particle Cannons to be effective. And to force *Crimson Firebird* to pick who they wanted to engage.

Because Captain Boru had noted something really effective in planning this. That Super-Cruiser, while it had a lot of Heavy Particle Cannons to punch another cruiser with, only had four defensive Particle Cannons in single turrets and a single Railgun Pulsar for point-blank defense.

He could throw ten missiles at a time at them. Granted, most of the shards would miss, having separated at burnout, but he'd specifically ordered the first salvo to be loaded with the meanest stuff they had. *Gauntlet* only had a few Nines, being heavy on Sixes for engaging larger vessels. *Arkwright* was almost entirely loaded with Nines.

Kyushu had Twelves. Normally not nearly as effective against big ships, but a Super-Cruiser traded armor and toughness for speed and offensive firepower. If she'd have brought a Line Cruiser, Nafizul didn't think this trick would work.

"Gunner, a reminder," Captain Boru said behind him. "Enemy marshal is trained as a bodyguard and bureaucrat, per briefing materials. The only naval expert she had is currently a prisoner on this vessel, after your cousin noted that she might be an assassin."

Bodyguard and bureaucrat. How to take advantage of that? Bodyguards were supposed to step into fire to protect their principal. Nafizul had actually loaded an armor-piercing slug into a rifle once, then fired the damned bullet through the first person in order to get the target.

So, aggressive. Bureaucrat, so deliberate and careful, rather than crazy.

Good thing he was bringing the crazy today.

Nafizul checked his boards and noted that everyone was following orders.

"Radio, have someone watch friendly turrets for one rotating aft to engage us from ambush," he added.

"On it," Magorian replied. "Also working ECM here with *Arkwright*."

Electronic Countermeasures. Static and noise to throw off targeting scanners. Anything to make a missile travel on the wrong intercept vector or have a plasma beam miss by however little it managed.

A miss was a miss.

"Light them up hard, Magorian," Captain Boru ordered. "Hold it as long as both of you can as we charge."

"Sir, yes, sir."

Nafizul had it plotted on his boards. Expectations. Reality. Maneuver vectors based on all those little esoteric things that Nyssa was apparently doing, because he couldn't remember a training simulation with this level of crisp detail.

They might even pull this off.

"I'm detecting salvoed missile fire from the enemy vessel," Nyssa announced.

Almost exactly on a timer Nafizul had in his head, for what it was worth. And part of the reason he let the three Escorts get ahead of him, because all of their tubes fired forward, so he'd see something turn long ways around to threaten *Marrakesh* if it turned into a double-cross.

"All defensive guns engage at maximum range and do not spare your barrels," Nafizul ordered.

Shortly, the tables would turn.

54

—————

Tom had listened to the planning. Boru had an ace up his sleeve, as long as the three other vessels didn't turncoat.

How in all the hells had that man not been assigned to a Line Cruiser? Except that he and Boru had talked about how Boru went from Knight to Commander to Captain in rapid sequence specifically to get this vessel out of mothballs when the latest war had suddenly exploded again.

Then someone had captured lightning in a bottle with this crew. Might even be enough to save his life today, because Ana Pera would probably put him up against the wall next to Arodd for a firing squad if she won.

Boru might be third, but he was under orders and a foreign national.

Might come down to how close it was if she did win.

He turned and made eye contact with sailor Farrell, quietly minding things in the corner.

Would she be called upon as an executioner today?

"What are they doing?" Arodd asked, quietly enough that Tom could ignore him if he wanted.

"Putting the Escorts on the front line to engage," Tom replied. "Spread out enough to overlap fire and force *Crimson Firebird* to pick who to shoot at. If they were smart, they'd start hammering us anyway, because we have the most firepower. Plus, if they knock us out, the other three probably surrender."

Arodd nodded when Tom looked back at him. Not a lot to say.

"Yasmin, anything we need to worry about?" he turned to his usually-quiet aide.

"Taggart has it nailed down pretty well, Tom," she replied. "Pera is sending orders to the Escorts, but Taggart cracked the whip on them and reminded them who the Supreme Autocrat was. Does it normally go down like this?"

"Emotionally, yes," Arodd replied. "Except in a boardroom or maybe over dinner, if you can poison them. I took out my immediate predecessor the old-fashioned way, by having him arrested and shot before any of his allies could react. It is a hard civilization. I think they could improve it by changing things to a long term in office. Say ten or twelve years. Then letting the old fart retire to Emeritus. Couldn't do it here, but that was the pack of hyenas I had accumulated around me. That, and being done with the whole mess and wanting out."

"What happens if we win?" Yasmin asked him. "I'm willing to bet my next paycheck that she killed everyone before she left. If we kill her, have we just decapitated the *Tyranny* entirely?"

Tom hadn't made it that far in his logic, but yeah, that might be a problem.

"We do still have Irelyn Cayne in our possession," Tom offered as the others fell a little flat.

"Arodd, is she up to it?" Lynch asked, having largely stayed out of galactic politics today. "Do we need to deliver her to Grandingham, kiss her on both cheeks, and let her take over?"

Talk about a win by forfeit.

"Worse, I might be in a position to turn right back around and return to power in Zulou," Arodd mused. "Change enough things that I could retire, if the entire *Tyrannical House* is gone."

"You'd never escape again, Arodd," Tom reminded him. "They'd be watching and know this trick, so they'd likely kill you at the first hint of trouble."

"That's what keeps me moving, Tom," the man replied. "But let us get to a position of safety after Boru saves all our lives. Then we can figure out what to make of that future."

Tom grunted and turned back to his boards. The squadron had screamed a challenge and charged. At least metaphorically.

Time to see if they could pull it off.

55

Padraig liked his new Gunnery Officer, but today wasn't a day for half-measures, so he was going to stay more involved than he might have before. But then, Maddox had fought the ship like an extension of Padraig's will, and *Murderhobo* would have already gotten to point blank with the enemy.

"Gunner, we ready to fire?" he asked.

"Ten seconds, sir," Haque replied. "I think I have their reload cycle timed, which might let our Heavy Particle Cannons, us and *Gauntlet*, range for hull from here. No idea if we can hit, but it might be possible to catch a missile launching and damage it before it ignites."

Wing and a prayer, but Padraig could see the logic. Any little bit to chip away at the enemy as they closed.

"Tyrant Squadron, begin launching missiles now," Nafizul ordered. "Maintain sequence and notify me immediately if you have loading troubles. Stay with your smallest until you use them up, as we're trying to damage and capture a pirate vessel threatening the future of the *Enlightened Tyranny of Traisa*."

Padraig grinned at that. Probably a load of horse shit, but it would look good later. And if they lost, those Escorts could play that order back and hope it was enough to save their careers.

Unlikely, but anything was possible.

Aft, two tubes immediately burped. Flanks, launching sideways by using a small electromagnetic catapult to thrust the missile into open space, where it would count to five, rotate on gyros to the programmed heading, and ignite thrusters. Burn until it hit speed, then separate into six or nine pie slices of solid steel moving at high speed.

Explosives wouldn't have added much to the overall effectiveness, and made them more fragile.

It took defensive Particle Cannon fire to really knock them off course with physics. Galactic billiards.

If you could.

"Radio, what's he doing with his turrets?" Padraig asked, unsure if Nyssa or Bex would answer.

"Adjusting now, sir," Bex said. "They were all set to broadside us at range, and suddenly started doing math."

As in, four defensive turrets attempting to engage eighty or ninety shards inbound. Scatter would mean that most missed, but someone was shining a light in their eyes with all that Scout ECM, so they would be hard pressed to identify which ones were a true threat.

Conversely, his force was all small guns that were optimized to engage and defeat incoming missiles, as long as everyone coordinated fire.

And as long as he could trust them. Which was honestly about as far as he could throw one of those hulls barehanded.

But they launched. And six missiles tracked forward and true, matching the two pairs *Marrakesh* had behind them as a staggered wave.

All the more to confuse gunners, if things were coming constantly and you might lose track of something.

The hull rang like a lunch bell rung in the distance.

"Ranging fire, Padraig," Chance called from her station aft. "Glancing blow. Damage control inspecting."

"Stay on it, Chance," Padraig said.

Things had been so whirlwind that he's spent most of his time getting Haque up to speed and taking care of his various guests, but she had him backstopped.

That might be the difference today, because that Super-Cruiser could hit them from here with a lot more turrets than he could counter with.

"Mister Haque, ranging fire," Padraig ordered.

56

Nafizul nodded, getting a feel for the rhythm. It was like lining up your shot through a glass spotting scope as the target walked down the street, watching him wobble back and forth just enough that you had to time it just right.

Pull the trigger. Hammer fall. Powder ignites. Bullet accelerates and leaves the barrel at supersonic or hypersonic speeds. Travels downrange. Intersects the target, who has been rocking back and forth as he walks.

Do it wrong and maybe puncture a lung or carom oddly off a rib. Hurt, but a chance for medical intervention to save a life if experts got to him fast enough.

Do it right and he's already dead by the time he falls over, heart completely ruptured inside his chest and unable to do anything. Still possible to save him, but one hell of a lot more complicated and far shorter windows to pull it off.

Starships dueling took him back to that street. Two ships, each moving on their own vector, attempting to wiggle and dance in any way that might throw off aim. Bright lights shined electronically in enemy eyes to blind them and introduce any element of error.

Hell, even solar wind could impact a shot far enough away, but he'd specifically asked Nyssa and Zarah for a place outside any heliosphere to negate that. Slight advantage for gunners, but he'd rather his people be more accurate taking out shards, because he had the edge in missile combat and could survive cannon hits for a while.

"*Gauntlet*, rotate your heavy turret to engage pirate warship," he ordered on the squadron line. "Pod Team, make sure to provide additional coverage on that flank. All vessels, maintain missile fire."

Because the *Traisan* sailors were a lot more likely to follow his orders if they thought that the Transport with the Escort Pod was protecting their asses.

Not a lot of firepower in front of him to take on a Super-Cruiser, but enough to hold some line. To negate his missiles and overwhelm him with shards, because *Marrakesh* had four twin batteries on the corners by herself, plus seven more Particle Cannons on the others. Fifteen cannons to engage ten launchers.

He could afford letting his heavies slug it out, because *Crimson Firebird* had to use his own heavies defensively or he'd be eating steel.

"Gunner, give him a pair of Threes," Captain Boru ordered sharply. "Next salvo."

Nafizul wanted to ask, but autopilot had him typing to the loading crews aft. And Boru had a rep as a good fighting captain, so maybe he'd seen something.

"Threes loading," Nafizul announced. "Firing now. Heavy turret, adjust your aim down and right a shade."

Nothing that jumped out at him, save that he was on that

street again, tracking that target prior to executing him with extreme prejudice.

Then they fired the Heavy Particle Cannon and something over there fluoresced.

"Radio, what just happened?" he asked, still typing orders and watching screens.

"I'm detecting a secondary explosion, sir," Magorian announced. "Might have caught a missile half out of the tube and caused it to ignite. Tracking a corkscrew on that flank."

Pure luck, but sometimes you got that. He knew *Marrakesh* couldn't woodpecker their way through that armor quickly. Even the lighter casing on a ship like that, to say nothing of anything heavier. But if a missile's rocket systems went off in the tube, you might have a blowtorch on your hands in the middle of a lot of fragile systems.

"Radio, track missile launch rate on that flank and let me know if it falls off," he ordered. "Heavy turret, shift your shooting in a little but stay on plane."

Maybe the armor over there was damaged. Maybe they could slip a shot through a hole in the hull. *Marrakesh* was taking a bit of a beating from incoming fire, but the enemy commander had made the dumbest mistake Nafizul could think of, spreading their fire out across all four warships instead of hammering them into the mud sequentially.

Bodyguard and bureaucrat. Not a sailor.

Only a killer metaphorically, knowing *Traisa*. Might not have killed anyone herself in years, not counting prisoners tied to chairs for interrogation or folks lined up for a firing squad.

Mindset.

"Gunner, I'm not detecting any missile launches on his port side," Magorian called. "Only starboard."

Nafizul nodded. If she'd just lost half her launchers, she was in a lot of trouble.

"Escort Squadron, rotate all of your fire onto the pirate," Nafizul ordered. "Pod team, you are responsible for protecting everyone until I say otherwise. Gun teams, you, too. Everyone on *Marrakesh*, you are protecting our allies from a pirate. Make them look good."

Hopefully, nobody pulled anything, rolling their eyes at him for that sort of a speech, but it felt right. Felt necessary.

And the Escorts had a chance to pay the big ship back for the abuse they'd been taking. *Kyushu* wasn't dead, but they'd been hammered twice with hits solid enough to penetrate armor and outer compartments, though they were still fighting.

"Helm," Captain Boru suddenly called. "Accelerate in and shift down and port about five degrees each. Roll to keep all turrets clear to engage *Crimson Firebird*. Gunnery teams, go for broke right now. Everything up to the edge of the cooling systems and hold it."

Nafizul watched, but didn't see what Boru had. But he'd seen something.

Oh. Shit. Those Threes. He'd lost track of them except as part of a larger shotgun blast of buckshot between the sides.

They'd separated. Four of them might be tracking close enough to matter to defensive gun teams.

And they were Threes. Triple the mass of the Nines he'd opened up the battle with. A whole hell of a lot harder to deflect, so those folks better rotate their Heavy Particle Cannons specifically to engage.

And *Marrakesh* was charging.

"Tyrant Squadron, follow us in," Nafizul ordered on the

team line. "Pirate vessel is in trouble and we can break them right now. Rapid fire all weapons as you bear."

Always a risk that someone chose this moment to put a shot into his ass, but that would make them enemy combatants, right at the moment when *Marrakesh* was on the verge of winning the battle.

And *Marrakesh* had taken a lot less damage relative to mass than any of the others. Might be possible to crush all of them if he got a kill on *Crimson Firebird* and somebody got out of line.

What would that look like on an After-Action Report?

"I'm seeing a probable!" Magorian called.

Nafizul watched the screen and had to agree. One of those big Three shards was getting hit, but it was so close that the Particle Cannon firing had gone myopic and couldn't really focus effectively. And the ship wasn't moving fast enough to dodge.

He'd heard stories about that Leviathan *Marrakesh* had nearly killed, a couple of years ago.

Captain Boru was a lucky captain. And Nafizul was as superstitious as the next sailor.

He held his breath and watched, even as other shards tracked and cannon belched at one another.

Impact.

He'd never actually seen it in person. Only on videos of massed fleet actions where an overload had turned into an overwhelm.

It was like a bullet entering a chest, having traveled all that distance and intersected.

Heart or rib? That was the only question.

Mass and speed turned into friction transfer. Slower than a bullet. Armor plate designed to hold. At least as much as it could, like a plated vest someone had under their clothing.

Wasn't enough.

Bullet entered metal flesh. Plasma and atmosphere mushroomed outward from the wound.

Target collapsed on the street bleeding to death.

Lights went out on the hull as relays overloaded and systems cooked. Or got shattered.

"All gun teams, cease offensive fire," Nafizul ordered. "Everyone go fully defensive immediately to engage any missile shards left on the board. Keep your missile tubes loaded but hold your fire. Captain Boru, they might be done."

57

Padraig kept the smile off his face, maintaining a neutral intensity instead.

He'd have to ask Secretary Gelashvili, but at this point, *Marrakesh* might have more combat experience than ninety percent of a fleet at war. Expert crew. Excellent people.

And—since he was being honest with himself—a con job to radically upend the odds. But Torray had said that Padraig manufactured his luck.

"Radio, get me the enemy commander," he ordered.

"Stand by, sir," she replied. "I'm not getting anything coherent out of them at the moment."

Padraig wondered, but then a series of petite detonations walked down the side of the ship, like a pod of whales breeching and blowing air out.

"Bex, are those blow-out vents operating?" he asked.

"Sir, that's what it appears to be," she replied a moment later. "Secondary and tertiary explosions suggesting that a fuel line or a generator failed and they've lost all power. *Crimson Firebird* might be dead in space."

Padraig nodded. It happened. Something torqued at the wrong moment. Damage bled through bulkheads that should have held it. Should have stopped it. Vents failed to open to let off pressure.

Super-Cruisers sacrificed internal bracing and solidity for speed. Lighter so they could go faster.

There were costs associated with every decision you made in naval architecture. Sometimes they came back and bit you on the ass.

"Radio, have the Escorts sail close and stand by for emergency and rescue operations," Padraig ordered.

Then he paused and considered the situation.

"Supreme Autocrat, you may need to take command at this juncture."

<h1 style="text-align:center">58</h1>

Arodd had been expecting to die today. Several times over. Just waiting for a clue as to who would be holding the knife.

Might have been Irelyn. Greer Rownett or Taran Severt would have smiled. Ana had certainly intended to do the deed.

He reached down and muted the line to the bridge.

"Tom, is there any chance I could hire Boru away from you folks?" he asked, knowing the answer but only half jesting.

Because...

"None whatsoever, Arodd," Tom replied. "Keeping that boy. You understand why now."

And he did.

Arodd turned to sailor Farrell.

"Thank you," he said simply. "I do not believe I will be needing your services, Farrell. You may stand down."

"Aye, sir!" she said, smiling and already headed to the hatch.

He found Kaitlin Lynch.

"I'll likely to be up all night," he began.

"I've already got the kitchen staff running all out," she

replied. "If nothing else, the extra food can be served to sailors Padraig takes aboard."

"He would do that?" Arodd asked, blankly confused.

"He has done that," she replied sternly. "The Escorts might not have space to take on survivors if Padraig has just killed that ship."

"Then it appears as though I will be traveling to Grandingham after all," he mused. "The lie becomes the truth. How will we escape from that mess?"

"Do you want to?" Tom asked. "Nobody knows the truth except you, Arodd. Any story you wanted to share become definitive, because we'll never gainsay you."

"It's tempting, Tom," he admitted. "But, as you noted, I'd get sucked right back down into that morass of quicksand that is Household politics and never have a chance to escape again."

"Tell them that we're hauling you to whatever station is next along the border when you're ready, Arodd," Kaitlin told him. "Then turn away and run like hell for *A'Zedi*."

He blinked. Nodded. Pressed his lips together.

"Captain Moneaux, you sort that portion out and let me know how we're doing it," he ordered the woman. "Tom and I will be busy with the locals."

"Aye, sir," Moneaux replied.

Arodd took a deep breath and opened the line again.

"Attention, *Crimson Firebird*, this is the Supreme Autocrat. ***You will explain yourself.***"

59

Tom watched Arodd pull that cloak back on and turn himself into the man in charge. Almost a second identity, having spent a few days around him to see the man hidden inside.

"Supreme Autocrat, this is Third Officer Echeverría," a woman replied in a shaky voice. Shock. Raw, possibly from yelling at the top of her lungs. "Captain Gil and our passenger appear to have been lost to a bridge hit. We are currently attempting to reach them but the vessel has suffered significant damage and I have ordered a ship-side shutdown of power to fight fires and keep overloads from cascading. What are your orders, sir?"

Tom sat back and shook his head. Eggshell. Likely lost the entire bridge crew if a Third Officer was replying.

Casualties might be horrendous over there.

Arodd looked a little lost. Tom reached over and hit the mute button.

"This might be where you order them to send all non-critical crew to the Escorts, as well as all the lightly injured," he offered. "We might have the best medical facilities. Lynch?"

"Undoubtedly, Tom," she replied. "Ships that small might only have a medical corpsman and a sickbay with two beds. Nothing ready for a crisis of this scale."

Arodd nodded.

"Echeverría, you will take command of *Crimson Firebird* until relieved," the Supreme Autocrat intoned heavily. "Begin transferring all non-essential crew to my Escort squadron. *Marrakesh* will collect the severely injured for transport to Grandingham. Radio Officer Taggart, you will take charge of coordinating all five vessels. Additionally, send a message to the base at Grandingham ordering them to send repair and medical support to these coordinates immediately."

"Understood, Supreme Autocrat," Echeverría replied.

"Working now, sir," Taggart replied. "We're just about to launch both shuttles with medical teams aboard and I've let Doctor Hyden know."

Arodd tapped a button. He looked up and Tom wondered if the man had aged ten years in the last ten minutes, but recognized the weight of supreme command returning to his shoulders.

"Only for a day or two, Arodd," Tom reminded him. "Then you can be free."

"I'm relying on Boru's luck there, too, Tom," he replied.

60

Padraig watched shuttles run, hauling firefighting crews in and injured sailors out. The Escorts had all sailed close enough to string lines for most of *Crimson Firebird*'s sailors to cross safely

"Chance, what are things like aft?" he asked.

"Damage Control is on top of it, Padraig," she replied. "Only one hit penetrated significantly. Most of it shattered armor plate and punctured the outer ring of chambers, but they were designed to absorb that fire. We'll have everything fully pressurized again in about an hour."

"Stay with that and make sure Doc Hyden is ready for bodies," Padraig told her, then opened the shipwide intercom. "Security, contact the bridge."

"Farrell here, sir."

"Guests for dinner, Farrell," Padraig said. "Keep them entirely separate from Irelyn Cayne unless you get other orders from the Supreme Autocrat. Presumably, we'll be overflowing those empty cabins around Medical, so get all your people off their normal duties and suited up. We'll know more when help arrives from Grandingham."

"Already deploying my people, sir," she replied.

"Out."

Padraig truly appreciated Cam Farrell on days like this. Woman could have taken a promotion to officer if she'd wanted, but then she'd have a real job, instead of spending her days training. Still, she knew when to step up and handle things without instruction.

Like most of them.

He checked the clock. Just under an hour since *Crimson Firebird* had died. And, supposedly Ana Pera and Captain Gil, along with most of the bridge crew. Haque had mentioned a heart shot. This was more like a bullet between the eyes. Just as permanent.

"Radio, any news from Grandingham?" he asked.

"I invoked the Supreme Autocrat on what was supposed to be a surprise inspection, Captain," she replied. "Noted an attempted piracy raid that he destroyed, and ordered them to send a troop transport, a repair vessel, and their local flagship. They are falling over themselves to comply, but were not prepared to move quickly, so I expect we will not see them for a day."

"Order them to send those ships immediately on readiness, rather than coordinating a squadron, Taggart," Padraig ordered. "Have Torray sign it, but I need ships here now instead of pretty."

"Aye, sir. Will update them."

Padraig studied the plot. The scurrying back and forth.

"Mister Haque, you have the bridge," he announced. "I'll be consulting with the Supreme Autocrat."

Then he rose, and started aft.

61

———

Padraig found them in the flag bridge, but someone had baked cookies, so he stole one still warm and gooey as a reward for the bullshit his day had turned into.

"I got the message from Taggart, Boru," the Supreme Autocrat said as Padraig found a station and sat. "What are your intentions?"

"Turn over local operations to whoever arrives," Padraig told him. "Haul you to Grandingham and let you supervise whatever needs doing from there. Past that, I've been fighting."

"Captain," Moneaux interjected. "Kaitlin and I are working on a scam that gets him there, then we pull out and run lateral with comments on a second surprise inspection that will not be a surprise once the border fleets know he is about. We'll pick a spot and coordinate to rendezvous with a *Directorate* fleet in deep space."

"I'd ask if we could pull that off, but you are the Supreme Autocrat," Padraig turned back to the man. "What do we do with Irelyn Cayne?"

"Tom suggested that she might end up replacing me,"

Torray shrugged. "Assuming Ana killed everyone else before coming here to chase me down. I wouldn't have simply locked them up if I was leaving town suddenly."

"So the Household is destroyed for the moment?" Padraig asked.

"The bureaucracy survives," Torray said. "They do most of the work, with the various chiefs being political appointees that issue orders and execute my commands. But yes, there will be chaos."

"Marshal, is that to our benefit or detriment?" Padraig asked.

"What do you mean, Captain?"

"*Traisa* is generally neutral this time around," Padraig said. "War of the Fourth Alliance. Obviously, we're expecting a new Supreme Autocrat to take office. If that takes a significant amount of time, does *Traisa* descend into a civil war as various survivors suddenly lunge at an unexpected opening? Does the *Directorate* get involved or remain aloof? Does *Wronlori* meddle or try something like launching raids on *Traisan* worlds in the ensuing chaos?"

"All are likely outcomes, Boru," Torray said. "Did you have a better idea? I had not intended to leave this much pandemonium in my wake."

Padraig considered his words carefully, aware of Tom Ussher and Yasmin Moneaux watching.

"As I understand it, Irelyn Cayne might be the only senior member of your Household left, sir," he said. "Should she become the next Supreme Autocrat? Is she up for it? Does that make things better or worse?"

"How would you outrun her wrath from Grandingham?" Torray asked.

"You are the Supreme Autocrat, sir," Padraig offered. "Your

word is law in the *Enlightened Tyranny of Traisa*. Invite *A'Zedi* to send a fleet to Grandingham for whatever reason, then you board the flagship and renounce your title in her favor. Or somebody's. They'd be far less likely to start something facing a fleet. Especially after we've just smashed a Super-Cruiser with a Tactical Transport. Then we get you to safety."

He watched the man parse that, lips pursed and eyes distant.

"Yes," he decided. "Tom, have Taggart summon your people to meet us at Grandingham. In the open and let them know that they will have whoever you were meeting. And to behave. I will talk to Irelyn privately and see how she feels about her options."

Padraig nodded. Let the big players sort it out and he'd get all this craziness off his deck the sooner.

"Oh, and Boru?" Torray said as Padraig started to turn away. "You will be my flagship as we depart Grandingham. I'm not about to sail on a less lucky ship while I have you around."

Padraig shrugged.

"As you've noted, sir, we manufacture our luck sometimes."

"Which is exactly why I want you close."

62

Padraig was back in the waiting room. *A'Zedi* Intelligence Services, in its own building on Horwin not far from Fleet Command. Best day uniform, so no medals. Nothing standing out beyond Captain's rank and *Marrakesh* patch. Nothing more needed.

The room had not changed. The civilians behind the counter had not changed. He'd been here enough times to even recognize a few of them, but they displayed no familiarity and never smiled.

All older. All stern. Civilian, and they didn't care what your military rank was because you couldn't give them orders.

Padraig had arrived a little early, because that was always better than a little late. Settled and meditated on the colors in here, how the mix of white and mulberry paint and tiles went well with his uniform. Old wooden pews from when this had been a space where general service officers came to receive orders, before Line Command had leveled a couple of old buildings and built a sleek new headquarters a generation ago.

The spies had happily taken this building over in turn.

A door opened behind the counter and the Permanent First Secretary, Madam Mariami Gelashvili, appeared.

"Captain Boru, could you join me?"

He was up and moving, following her deeper into the building to an office with a number but no name. Same as usual, her behind a clean desk and him at attention on this side. He was not prepared for Marshal Ussher to be sitting already.

"Captain, sit," she gestured.

Ussher grinned. Padraig settled in beside him.

"Tom?" she asked.

Padraig had a hard time seeing a Division Marshal on such terms, but he was just a captain around here.

"Boru, Arodd Torray wanted me to convey to you his personal thanks for saving his ass and getting him out of the *Enlightened Tyranny of Traisa* in one piece," Ussher began. "At present, it looks like Irelyn Cayne will succeed as Arodd's replacement, but that might take a year. You and *Marrakesh* will not be sailing anywhere near *Traisan* space for a long time, not that you would be surprised at that."

"Assumed so, sir," Padraig replied.

"However, I did come bearing gifts," Ussher grinned again. "Mariami?"

Padraig turned as the tall woman reached back and grabbed two packages from a credenza. One both flat, with one being about the side of his hand and the other perhaps as big as his chest.

"Open the small one first," she instructed.

Padraig was mystified, but complied. Inside was one of those jewelry boxes that held necklaces. Hinged at the top, so he flipped it open and saw a gold five-pointed star on a red ribbon.

"Hero of the Tyranny, sirs?" he asked, looking up at both of them.

"The highest award the Supreme Autocrat can award, for either civilian or military personnel," Tom Ussher acknowledged. "Equivalent to the *A'Zedi* Medal of Valor and superior to an Order of Merit. That will have place of honor on your dress uniform when you are formal, Boru."

He supposed so. There were only a handful of awards like it, and Ussher had just mentioned two of them. Medal of Valor winners rated a salute from anyone they encountered, up to and including the Grand Marshal of the Fleet herself.

His next Founding Day dinner ought to be interesting.

Padraig closed the box carefully and set it to one side. The larger box was a uniform carrier, once he got the top loose from the bottom.

Dark green. *Traisan* Green, once his brain processed it. It was the three stars on the collar that didn't compute.

Then he thought about it and shrugged. The man had ordered him to assume the rank of Fleet Commander in order to deal with both Mistress at Arms Pera and the squadron of warships that had arrived from Grandingham. And Torray had personally instructed all of his people—while they'd still been his—to treat him as such.

It made him roughly the equivalent of an *A'Zedi* Fleet Marshal. Or Tom Ussher's superior. Technically.

Still didn't compute.

"For obvious reasons, it is not something you will normally wear, even with dress uniform occasions," Ussher was saying. "At the same time, there will be circumstances when it might be appropriate. I have no idea what they might be at present, but I also presume that you will retire from *A'Zedi* service at some point, so you might have a use for it."

Padraig couldn't help the scowl he directed at the man.

"I will remind you, Boru, that the new Supreme Autocrat does like you," Madam Secretary interjected. "There was a note from her that accompanied this package."

"This came from Supreme Autocrat Cayne?" Padraig asked, shocked entirely sideways now.

"Arodd Torray sent her a letter requesting the two for delivery to the *A'Zedi* Ambassador on Zulou, who conveyed them here," she nodded. "She included a letter offering her thanks and congratulations. I will remind you that she would have died on *Marrakesh* had Pera destroyed it. And Pera would have. Additionally, she notes that you spoke up for her with Torray, suggesting that she be installed as his replacement at a point where he was in his rights to have Cameron Farrell execute her."

"It was that, or watch the *Enlightened Tyranny of Traisa* possibly collapse into civil war, sir," Padraig replied.

"Not every officer would have seen that, Padraig," she told him. "Fewer would have done something to stop it, instead of helping it along. The *Directorate* obviously can't reward you publicly for these actions without letting too many people guess the truth about you, so we've added certain notations in your file. If and when you do retire from sailing for a desk job, there will be an Order of Liberty added to your regalia."

Padraig blinked at her owlishly, attempting to process that.

The Order of Liberty? The silver nine-pointed star with the blue cross fleury at its centre, along with a fuchsia sash worn across the chest from the right shoulder?

The *Directorate* didn't do most of those knightly organizations that some places did, but it did maintain a handful of such groups. Membership in that order was second only to the Order of *A'Zedi* itself.

"Ma'am, I'm just trying to do my job as I see it best," he replied.

"Which is why you are in this office, Padraig," she replied, smiling. "And while Tom Ussher came along to deliver these packages and make sure that you understood how successfully you pulled off what might have been a serious fuckup. He told me that you manufacture your luck and I unfortunately laughed in his face, but I already knew that about your, Boru."

"I still think he might be better in a Line Cruiser, Mistress," Ussher spoke up.

"Absolutely not," she replied, still smiling. "Those sail in pretty squadrons and occasionally encounter hostile forces. Padraig Boru does so much more for me, as you've seen. I have no intention of letting you people have him back. Ever. I might, however, allow you to build him a new Tactical Transport. One of the P-boats, but it would have to be named *Marrakesh* in service, obviously."

Padraig managed to keep a straight face as he watched those two banter.

"Obviously," Ussher replied, then turned to Padraig. The smile was back. "How long until you retire, Boru?"

"How long until you pry me out of that station and make me, sir?" Padraig smiled back.

"Not anytime soon, Padraig," Madam Gelashvili spoke up. "In fact, as soon as you have your current repairs completed, I have a mission for you."

"Sir?" he asked.

"You have places to go, Boru," she nodded. "People and cargo to haul. Things to do to make this a better galaxy."

"Doing my best."

"Keep at it, Captain."

READ MORE

Be sure to read the rest of the Operation Marrakesh series!

https://www.knottedroadpress.com/product-category/science-fiction/operation-marrakesh

ABOUT THE AUTHOR

Blaze Ward is a prolific Indie writer and publisher who works mostly in Science Fiction and Light Thriller, with occasional forays into lots of other genres like superheroic fantasy.

You can find more of his titles at www.blazeward.com/books, www.KnottedRoadPress.com and wherever else you buy your books.

He also edits Boundary Shock Quarterly, an SF magazine he founded in 2018, and Thrill Ride Magazine.

ABOUT KNOTTED ROAD PRESS

Knotted Road Press publishes dynamic fiction set in exotic locations. Our authors cover a wide range of genres including science fiction, fantasy, mystery, literary, and poetry. We also have unique non-fiction voices in genres such as autobiography, business, cookbooks, and how-tos. We offer both DRM-free ebooks and print books for a global readership.

www.KnottedRoadPress.com